SWEET SAGE

Catherine Stebinger

This is a work of the imagination. All the characters and events portrayed in this novel are fictional.

For Allan

Prologue

The acquisition team had done its job well. Alex eased the sleek ebony BMW slowly down Main St. This town looked charming enough to be the set for an old Jimmy Stewart movie. Soft snow drifted lazily over slate rooftops as old-fashioned streetlamps spread a golden light over pine bough wreaths and festive shop windows. The team's report stated that the town was growing quickly despite the soft economy, thanks to all the Wall Street yuppies looking to own the requisite suburban *House and Garden* trophies. Only one store could cause a minor hiccup in the plan, and there it was, sitting across the street from the volunteer fire department, huge balsam wreaths adorning its front windows. No, he smiled to himself; this small business looked cute enough as a "mom and pop" operation... but it would not cause his company problems. It was fortunate his uncle had discovered that the irascible aging owner of these old buildings needed cash...fast. The buildings were charming. Linked together and modernized, they would provide enough space for his flagship store. He drove on with satisfaction to his uncle's house

Catherine Stebinger

Chapter 1

Olivia glanced up at the old wooden clock with its chubby baker boy hands hanging on the old brick wall. 5:30pm. She wiped out the last crumbs from the curved-glass bakery case. Closing time on Christmas Eve and yet the golden oak and red brick store buzzed with snow dusted customers vying for the very last of the glistening fruit tarts and crusty baguettes.

Harry, Olivia's floor manager, signaled silently that he was locking the doors. His usual impeccably groomed blonde hair stood on end, raked back by stressed fingers. His green bistro apron twisted to one side, the pockets bulging with notes, pens, and other hodgepodge gathered during the wild day's work.

With a smile and a feeling of deep satisfaction of a job well done, Olivia handed the last customer her box of pastries.

"You're a dear to have held these for me," said the white-haired woman holding her precious box. "I meant to come earlier, but you know how things happen." Leaning towards Olivia confidentially she whispered, "By the way, did I tell you that my nephew John, down at Planning and Zoning, told me that that big European Gourmet chain is looking for a place in town? Have you heard anything so ridiculous? They wouldn't last a minute here. And the way the economy has been, this town doesn't need two gourmet stores!"

Olivia's dark eyes widened in surprise. "No, you didn't mention it before, Mrs. Dunn."

"Oh! Well…I don't think he was supposed to have said anything to me about it! But, my dear, I'm sure you have nothing to worry about. John says they make their food in huge kitchens, and then drive it all over in big trucks to their stores. Nothing like what you do here. No one in this town will go to them, I can tell you. We all love your goodies!" she added, patting her box lovingly. "Now, keep this under your hat! John would never forgive me if he knew I told you anything. But, my dear, I just thought you ought to know."

Olivia tried to make sense of the gossipy elderly woman's words. Her golden day dimmed just a bit as she wondered whether to believe it.

"Oh dear! I shouldn't have said anything. Now you're going to worry!" exclaimed Mrs. Dunn as she watched Olivia's smile fade. "Well, don't," she said trying to repair the damage she'd done. "Everything will turn out alright, I'm sure! Go home and have a good Christmas and forget everything I've just said."

"Thank you for the information, Mrs. Dunn," Olivia replied civilly. "I hope you have a wonderful time with your family tomorrow. Tell Mr. Dunn I said Merry Christmas."

Oblivious to the shock waves left behind, the older woman cheerfully walked out into the falling snow, while Olivia looked at her disappearing back.

She relocked the door with a sigh, turned around and saw Harry, his apron off, attacking the overflowing garbage cans while good naturedly prodding the rest of the staff to finish with the clean-up. She smiled. She would not let that witch get to her!

"Come on you slugs! Santa will pass by your houses if you don't get a move on! I have a hot date tonight and need to go home and make myself irresistible!" Harry sang out cheerfully.

A pretty, rosy-cheeked girl with a mane of dark hair tied back with a bell bedecked Christmas ribbon smiled roguishly at him while washing out the coffee urns. "Who's it this time Harry, that cute new bartender over at Nickleby's?

"None of your business who it is, Lena. Let's just say he's hot, he's cute, and he's all mine....at least for tonight!"

Olivia smiled to herself and hoped that this time Harry would not get his feelings hurt as he had every time before. How he managed to pick exactly the wrong guy each time amazed her. In the six years she had known him, not one of his loves had worked out kindly.

She went into the kitchen to retrieve a bag she had hidden in one of the refrigerators. The bag of bottles clinked as she walked back to where the staff was cleaning. "To my amazing co-workers; I have a little holiday cheer and a thank you for working so hard. Sweet Sage has had a fantastic season thanks to all of you. A bottle of champagne to one and all to help celebrate, and a little something in an envelope to help keep you warm," she grinned handing out the gifts. "Merry Christmas, everyone!"

"OMG! I can't believe it's over!" Harry cried out, twirling in the middle of the floor with his champagne bottle as a dance partner.

Olivia laughed. "Not quite. We still have New Years. Let's finish up and get out of here."

"Race you to the finish!" crowed Harry heading over to the broom closet.

An hour later the store shone, neat and clean. Laughter and calls of "Merry Christmas!" hung in the air as the staff finished up and put on jackets.

Lena lagged behind the weary crew leaving out the back door. She enveloped Olivia in a bear hug punctuated by the jingle of the tiny bell in her hair.

"What would I do without you, Lena?" smiled Olivia hugging her in return. "Get some rest tomorrow. Merry Christmas."

"Merry Christmas to you, too." Lena rolled her eyes as a car in the parking lot beeped impatiently. "Hey, Harry, looks like you're ride is here. You sure you want to go out with him? I could tell him to leave."

"Very funny. Tell him I'll be right there."

Lena smiled impishly and waved good-bye.

Harry, one foot out the door, looked back at his boss and friend. She had worked harder and longer than anyone else had since Thanksgiving and should have been dancing a jig right now. Instead, she looked singularly alone standing in the doorway. "I guess I better not keep him waiting. You're not still going to help with your friend's party, are you? Want to hang out with me and my hot date, instead?"

Olivia shivered in the icy wind blowing through the doorway. She looked fondly at her dear right hand man and smiled. "You're very sweet Harry, but I think three's a crowd. Don't worry about me; I'll be fine. I promised Dan I'd help with his work party tonight, and I'm going to. But tomorrow…tomorrow's another story! I'm going to stay in my jammies all day, do nothing but drink hot cocoa, and watch old movies. Now get going. You don't want your hot date to be stolen!"

Persistent honks emitted from the idling car. "Well… Merry Christmas, sweetie! See you Tuesday." Harry gave her a big hug and pulled the door shut against the wind.

Olivia locked up behind him and walked back into the silent store. She stood still, a slight figure in the quietly creaking old building. Her thick mahogany hair was caught in a loose knot by a deep red scarf tied into a big floppy bow. Escaped tendrils softly framed her oval face. She looked younger than her thirty-two years, despite the smoky blue circles of fatigue under her eyes.

Listening to the sound of the humming refrigerator compressors, Olivia let her eyes roam over her small treasured business. It meant everything to her…stability, a sense of belonging, purpose, and friendship. She thought about Mrs. Dunn's bit of gossip and wondered if it was true. The impact on her business would be horrifying, if it was. She shook her head. This would not do. She wouldn't let gossip mar her joy and satisfaction of having made a success of her store. It had been a hard fought battle and she'd just about won. Her staff felt like the family she'd never had, the community had accepted her as one of their own, and her innovative cooking and astute business sense had led them to profitability two years ahead of schedule. What more could she possibly want? There was so much to celebrate, so much to be grateful for…and two days off to enjoy! With a smile, she quickly finished closing the registers and went downstairs to the office to tuck away the day's proceeds into the safe.

Olivia glanced at the clock again and realized she had very little time to run home and change before going over to Dan's house to help with his party. Fatigue washed over her in a wave as she thought of staying up late and making small talk with strangers she most likely would never see again. But… Dan was her dearest friend, and she'd do anything for him. He'd been there over and over again for her, ever since her fiancé Michael had died in a plane crash six years ago.

She grabbed her heavy black woolen coat and threw it on, tied a fluffy crimson scarf around her neck, and stepped out the back door into the cold night air. It was snowing harder now as she locked the door behind her. She patted the building affectionately and headed up the hill to her car.

    As she brushed the snow off her old Volvo, she noticed a big black BMW slowly cruising by the store. She looked closely to see if the driver was a customer who had forgotten something, but didn't recognize the man barely visible through the gloom. Ridiculously, a sense of unease gripped her. She finished wiping the windshield and got into her car, locking the doors. She watched as the BMW turned around and came by for another slow look. Finally, it drove off down the road. She thought of calling the police… but to say what? That a strange car was driving slowly in a snowstorm? Honestly! Now she knew she was losing her mind!

    Slowly Olivia shifted the car into reverse, backed out of her parking space, then cautiously drove down the hill. With her mind in a tired jumble, she mechanically drove through the now nearly empty streets to the outskirts of town where her stone cottage nestled at the edge of the state park behind the old Meres mansion.

Chapter 2

The light Olivia had left burning twinkled welcomingly out of her living room window as she drove into her driveway, making it less unpleasant for her to come home alone in the dark. She pressed the button on the visor to open the garage door, eased the car in, and sighed as the car came to a stop.

Olivia turned the car off and sat very still for a moment, feeling utterly unable to move. Exhaustion oozed out of every pore. She felt the weariness open the cracks to the old pains. Old hurts that were always ready to come flooding to the forefront when the defenses were down. All her clear headedness, independence, and strength seemed to recede like the tide, leaving her emotions bare and vulnerable. She thought of the years her mother had worked so hard raising her by herself, her father having disappeared soon after learning she was on the way. How exhausted her mother must have been, though she never showed it. Her mother had been a junior in college when she had met her father at a party. For a while, they had seemed fated to be together forever…but then her mother got pregnant. He fled, transferring to another college, never to see her mother again. Her mother's family, outraged by her situation, refused to have anything more to do with her. So…her mother left college and went to work cooking in restaurants. The two of them lived in a small studio apartment above a florist shop just off the bus line. Olivia and her mother did everything together until, at the age of eighteen, just as Olivia was to enter college, another bombshell exploded. Her mother was diagnosed with breast cancer – stage four. A year later she was gone, leaving Olivia alone. Olivia had been waiting tables at the restaurant where her mother was the chef. Needing to work full-time, she asked to be given a chance to work in the kitchen. Instead of going to college, she began a job to support herself that quickly turned into a passion. She met Michael and Dan when they came into the restaurant with dates one night. She had been walking through the dining room, when a laughing Michael spotted her and called her over to ask her about the dish they had just eaten. Michael never took his eyes off her the whole time she talked. When she finished her explanations, she turned around to leave, only to have Michael grab her hand and ask her name. Shyly, she had responded, then escaped back to the safety of the kitchen. Michael came back day after day, until she agreed to go out on a date with him. In a few short months, she had agreed to marry him. They were to get married right after he finished presenting his research at a conference in Germany. It was Dan who had come in, just as she was ending her shift and about to go to the airport, to tell her Michael's plane had crashed with everyone on board believed to be dead. It was Dan who took care of her as she grieved uncontrollably for months after. Dan, who became her best friend...and who now had a party to give with her help.

Olivia gathered what energy she had left and hit the button again to close the garage door. She stepped out of her car and gave herself a mental shake as she walked through the little mudroom into the kitchen. After putting a pot of strong coffee on to brew, she climbed the worn wooden staircase with its cheerful cabbage rose runner and headed for a hot shower.

The phone rang insistently as she stepped out of the tub. Olivia grabbed a thick white terry towel and made a mad dash for the phone, reaching it just as the answering machine turned on. Only one person could be calling on the landline at this time of night on Christmas Eve.

Dan's voice came pleadingly over the line. "Olivia! Thank God! My guests are going to be here any minute and nothing's ready! I totally burned the first tray of thingies you made for me and the bar's not set up! When are you coming over?"

Olivia had to laugh. This was so Dan. Here he was, one of New York's most competent, brilliant young corporate attorneys, but take him out of his element, and he was as insecure and disorganized as a young puppy surrounded by six neighborhood tomcats.

"Hang on, Dan. Let me turn this answering machine off. Now - relax! It's only six forty-five. Aren't your guests supposed to arrive around eight? I'm just changing and then I'll be right over. Go put some music on and stay out of the kitchen until I get there."

A windy sigh came through the receiver. "You're right. This party is making me crazy. What do you suppose possessed me to put it on? What if everyone is bored and hates it?" Another thought struck him. "What if no one comes?"

"Dan! Stop it! It'll be fine! If you relax and have a good time, everyone else will, too. And of course, they're coming! Now let me get dressed. Go pour yourself a drink, and I'll be right over before you know it." Olivia felt like a responsible sister taking care of a charming, but inept brother.

She put down the receiver and stood there a moment looking around her warm terra cotta tiled kitchen, wishing she could just curl up in the rocking chair with a good book. Instead, there was barely enough time to gulp down some coffee and get dressed.

A short time later she let herself into Dan's sleek modern house. Jazz played softly in the background and a gas fire burned brightly in the spectacular white marble fireplace. The white on white living room was neat as a pin, with deep red poinsettias in angular steel cachepots adding startling crimson accents. Dan's housekeeper Nora was a treasure, reflected Olivia.

She hurried to the kitchen, spurred on by sounds of clanking pans and voluble swearing. The scene in the stainless steel and marble kitchen belied the cool peace of the living room. Sheet pans, potholders, and boxes of prepared hors d'oeuvres lay on every surface. Dan, looking like a tall, befuddled owl in the middle of a disaster, stood by the open oven door, an oven mitt covered hand holding a tray of smoking and charred miniature pastries.

Though the restaurant-sized hood over the stove blasted away on high, smoke filled the kitchen and threatened to encroach upon the rest of the house, most likely to set off every fire alarm in its path. Quickly Olivia opened wide the kitchen windows and the back door leading to the terrace. She ran over, took the pan out of Dan's hand, and assessed whether anything was salvageable. It was grim.

Dan had a smudge on the cheek of his pale narrow face and his wire rim glasses had slipped down his aquiline nose. His deep blue eyes peered ruefully over the fogged glasses. "I thought I'd try one more tray, but as you can see, it wasn't a good idea."

Olivia just shook her head and smiled wryly. "What am I going to do with you? Okay. Let me see what I can do with what's left. Get out of the kitchen. Scoot!"

Though distracted, Dan couldn't help but notice how striking Olivia looked tonight. Somewhere in the back of his mind, he knew she had to be tired, but the corners of her eyes still crinkled with a smile, her shiny hair fell softly around her face to her shoulders in soft waves, and her simple black cocktail dress accentuated every beautiful curve of her body. He yearned to feel her softness against him and it took all his willpower not to swallow her in his arms. He knew only too well how she felt about him.

Bent over the oven, Olivia instructed crisply, "Go wash your face, then come back and set up the bar in the dining room. I'll take over here." Blind to the longing in his eyes, she found an apron, tied it on, and set to work creating order out of chaos. Reluctantly, Dan landed back in reality and headed off to obey orders.

In no time, Olivia had the remaining hors d'oeuvres warm and golden, set attractively on silver trays in the dining room. She set bowls of spiced nuts, a basket of freshly cut vegetables and dip, bread sticks, and mounds of shrimp in a cut glass bowl about the living room.

The smoke having dissipated, Olivia closed the windows and doors, took her apron off and went to find Dan. She found him filling the crystal ice bucket that stood in the center of a marble self-service bar. Bottles of wine, sparkling water, juices, and top shelf bottles of liquor stood waiting at attention by the rows of assorted glasses and stacks of colorful cocktail napkins. He gave her a relieved smile. Eight o'clock and all was well.

Now that his panic had subsided, Dan could not help but notice the blue rings of fatigue under Olivia's eyes. Overwhelming guilt hit him.

"Oh, Olivia, what have I done to you?" he said, reaching for her.

Olivia, too tired to protest, let herself be held. She closed her eyes and felt herself relaxing tiredly as Dan swayed gently back and forth to the soft jazz playing in the background. Memories of Michael drifted through her mind, of a time just before they were to be married...when life was amazingly simple and wonderful.

Dan felt her body relax against his and looked down. Her eyes were closed as though asleep. Dreamily, he nuzzled the dark curls on the top of her head with his lips, moving down slowly to nibble the top of her ear.

Olivia stiffened and quickly pulled out of his arms. "Dan..."

He froze. "Don't say anything. I know. I'm sorry..."

Like a scene out of a movie, the doorbell rang. Both of them just stood there looking at each other, pain in their eyes. When the doorbell rang a second time, Dan straightened his shoulders and left to answer it.

Olivia stood there, paralyzed. She wished she could return Dan's feelings the way he needed them returned. She loved him dearly... but not that way. But, what was romantic love, anyway? They were best friends. Couldn't romantic love develop over time? Impatiently, she shook her head. She did not need or want that kind of relationship...or to get married, for that matter. She was happy with their friendship and the store filled all her desires. It was Dan who needed more, but he would have to find that elsewhere.

Jovial voices boomed through her thoughts. Olivia shook herself and opened her eyes to see a short pudgy man with frizzled orange hair strut into the living room, his arm in possessive control of the waist of a very young and shapely blonde woman wearing stiletto heels, a bright red dress, and garish blue eye makeup.

As other guests began to fill the room around them, Olivia could not help but notice the tentative look on the young woman's face. It was clear she felt out of her element. Olivia went over to her, ignored the man, and smiled. "Welcome. I'm glad you could come. I'm Olivia." Without allowing his date to respond, the man shoved out a fleshy hand, grabbed Olivia's and pumped it vigorously. Loudly, he announced, "I'm Robert Morgan, and this is Tiffany. Very nice to meet you. Nice house you have here. Must have cost a pretty penny! Dan didn't tell me he had a girlfriend." He winked dramatically at her. "Why the big secret? I wouldn't mind waking up to you in the morning!"

Olivia smiled coldly. "There is no secret. Dan and I are just very good friends who go back a long way."

Olivia kicked herself for feeling she needed to explain herself to this odious little man. Really!

Feeling sorry for Tiffany and wondering how she had gotten mixed up with this jerk, she took her by the elbow and guided her over to the bar to offer her something to eat and drink. The room had now filled up, yet Olivia could still hear Robert's voice booming rude questions as he attacked unsuspecting fellow guests.

She left Tiffany talking quietly to a pregnant young woman and went back to mingle with the other guests who had just entered.

Olivia moved through the crowd introducing herself, working her way towards the front door where Dan still greeted newcomers. As she approached the dimly lit chandeliered foyer, her eyes were automatically drawn to the tall, singular man with the craggy face standing in the doorway. Somehow, he seemed vaguely familiar. She stopped for a moment to study his face, trying to place him…when he turned and looked directly into her eyes. His steely gray eyes raked over her face, holding her eyes in a challenging stare. It was as though he was clinically analyzing her worth for a future purpose. Her stomach gave a small lurch as she returned the stare, wondering at his audacity. Was he daring her to turn away first? Anger stirred in her as she returned the look with an equally challenging glare. Her hackles had been raised and she would not back down.

Olivia felt somewhat victorious when he was forced to look away. An older man next to him had just turned to introduce him to Dan. Released, Olivia let out the breath she had not realized she'd been holding. Immediately she changed direction and headed towards the kitchen to refill hors d'oeuvres in an attempt to regain her bearings.

At the door and out of Olivia's hearing, the older man was saying, "I didn't think you'd mind, Dan, if I brought along a nephew of mine to your party. He's here in town on business over the holidays and had nowhere to go tonight. Couldn't let him think we were unfriendly in this part of the world. Alex, this is Dan Spencer, one of the brightest attorneys in the stable. Dan this is my nephew Alex Dumaurier, CEO of European Gourmet."

"A pleasure to meet you, Alex", said Dan, gripping his hand firmly. "European Gourmet? I hear your company is growing by leaps and bounds in the Midwest."

"Well, I'm not sure what you've heard, but yes, it's been doing well."

"How's business in this economy?"

"It's a tough economy right now, but I think we're well positioned for growth. In some ways, other people's misfortunes are a blessing for us. We're able to take advantage of the low real estate prices to place ourselves in towns we might not have been able to move into so easily before." Alex gave a perfunctory smile. Somehow, he didn't feel like talking business right now. Time enough for that later. "How are you enjoying living in this town?" he asked, deftly changing the subject.

"I love it. I never thought I'd like living out of Manhattan, but I've got to tell you, this town is world class and has everything a person might need, including some pretty amazing food. You can sample some of it right here tonight," Dan said with pride, his eyes searching for Olivia. Spotting her he said, "Let me introduce you to the best chef in the world. And not only is she a great chef, but she has a pretty cool head for business, as well. You two should have a lot to talk about."

Dan led Alex and his uncle over to the table where Olivia was arranging tiny golden triangles of warm pastry on a three-tiered silver stand.

Olivia noticed Dan moving towards her with the two men. The stranger's eyes met hers for the second time and the corners of his stern mouth softened a little in the suggestion of a smile as they approached each other. That tiny change transformed the angular planes of his face. He appeared even more striking than before, with a hint of gentleness, though his eyes remained as guarded and cool as ever. Olivia's stomach performed another dance as she again met his probing look.

"Olivia, I'd like you to meet my boss, Leo Barbier and his nephew Alex Dumaurier. Alex is alone in town on business, so Leo thought it would be friendly to bring him by," introduced Dan, oblivious to the sparks flying about him. "Leo, Alex, I'd like you to meet my favorite person and the world's best chef, Olivia Caron. She owns the most fabulous gourmet store in town. Olivia, you and Alex should have a lot to talk about. He owns a gourmet food store, too, that's just a little bit bigger than yours. It's called European Gourmet," Dan laughed. "But you better watch out, Alex. The way Olivia is going, she may be your biggest competitor one of these days!"

Alex's eyes regained their steeliness and Olivia's eyebrows rose as she heard Dan's words.

Their hands met in polite greeting and Olivia willed herself not to flinch.

"It's nice to meet you," she miraculously heard herself say steadily and coolly. His hand felt warm in hers, with rough calluses on the palm. Did his hold have to send zaps of electricity straight to parts that had not been alive in years? Here was the enemy, in the flesh.

"Likewise," responded Alex slowly, taking her measure.

Olivia tried to pull her hand away, but Alex held on. She raised her dark eyebrows, questioning. He ignored the look and continued holding her work-worn hands. "Dan's right. We most probably have a lot to talk about."

"Possibly. Now could I please have my hand back?" she asked with a touch of asperity. Alex laughed and released her hand.

Dan looked at the two of them in mild puzzlement. Olivia quickly turned to Mr. Barbier, who had been watching the two of them with interest. She gave him her hand in greeting as well, only to have it swallowed up by both of his. "It's always a pleasure to meet a beautiful woman. Alex, we should invite this young woman to lunch with us one of these days."

"Thank you, Mr. Barbier that would be wonderful, I'm sure, but unfortunately lunch is a very busy time for me at the store. Maybe we can get together at some other time. Meanwhile, let me invite you to have a bite to eat here."

"No, no young lady. I won't take no for an answer. We'll catch up with you one of these days. We may have some business to talk over with you that might just interest you."

Olivia looked over at Dan. Dan shrugged his shoulders, not having a clue what was going on. She glanced back at Alex, whose eyes were more guarded than ever. Alarm bells sounded in her mind. Angrily, she swung back to Mr. Barbier.

"This business wouldn't have anything to do with European Gourmet coming into town by any chance?"

He gave her a pat on the cheek, and said, "There's nothing to be alarmed about. Any business we would have to talk over with you would be to your great advantage. But, now's not the time to even think about it. Why don't you come over and show me where the drinks are?" Dan quickly stepped in. "My apologies Leo. I'm being remiss as the host. Come right this way. Alex, will you join us?"

"Thank you, Dan, in just a minute."

Alex watched his uncle go off in search of a scotch on the rocks, then turned back to Olivia. An uncomfortable silence stretched between them for what seemed like an eternity.

Olivia gathered her wits and challenged him directly. "So. You are from European Gourmet."

"Yes." Alex replied, attempting to ignore the magnetic attraction he felt.

"Are you going to try to put me out of business?"

"We never set out to put anyone out of business. This country was built on competition. I provide nothing but opportunity."

Olivia felt a momentary panic, then fury. She knew her business was very well regarded in town, but she certainly did not have the buying power or capital behind her of a national chain like European Gourmet. But, damn it! None of that mattered. She was going to give him a run for his money. She looked at him, mink eyes blazing. "Then competition is what you are going to get. You better give it your best shot because I am not about to lose." Olivia spun around and stalked into the kitchen. Alex watched her disappear, as unwanted feelings stirred deep inside.

Dan glanced quizzically at Alex as he passed by him on his way to the kitchen, two steps behind Olivia. "Hey, are you alright? You looked like a virago blowing through the room!"

"Dan, did you know that Alex Dumaurier is going to bring a European Gourmet store into town? Did Mr. Barbier tell you about this?" she asked angrily.

"Whoa! No, I had no idea. And, are you sure those are his plans? You just met him."

"I'm ninety-nine percent sure. He just about said so right now. But, I'm going to fight it with everything I've got."

"I was wondering what was going on with the both of you. Look, do you want to go home? You must be done in and being here with him does you no good."

"Thanks Dan. I am flat out exhausted, but there's no way in hell I'm going home now. I don't want that man to think he already has me beaten." She picked up some hors d'oeuvres and walked back out of the kitchen with her chin in the air.

Dan looked after her thoughtfully.

Throughout the evening, Alex found his eyes insistently zeroing in on Olivia as she moved about the room. He studied her from afar, noting her fresh beauty that set her apart from every other woman in the room. It was too bad her store was directly in the path of his incoming business, but... business was going to have to be business.

A sudden guffaw of raucous laughter interrupted his thoughts. Annoyed by the sound erupting from his obviously drunk uncle, he moved away and decided to sample some of the new hors d'oeuvres Olivia was bringing out of the kitchen. Purely as business research, he assured himself.

Olivia smiled coldly and offered him a warm sage and Fontina puff. Alex had to admit to himself that the puffs were delicious, better than many items they produced in his own stores and as good as anything he had eaten in France; but more than that, it was Olivia's smile that sent waves of heat shimmering through every cell of his body. Their fingers touched slightly as she handed him a cocktail napkin. Olivia pulled back her hand as though singed by a hot stove. Alex, studiedly ignoring Olivia's reaction, took the napkin, "These are delicious. Do they come from your store?"

    Olivia fought to act normally. "Thank you, yes. Our customers seem to enjoy them. We created them last year and they have become one of our best sellers." She moved to get past him to put the tray on the table. He blocked her way.

    "You know, there might be other ways to do business than trying to destroy each other."

    "Really? What do you expect me to do? Hand over my baby and become part of your conglomerate? I don't think so. Now please let me by."

    Alex refused to move. Instead, he took her wrist, removed the tray from her hands, set it on the table, and led her down the hall. Olivia did not want to make a scene, so quietly followed until they were out of sight, then yanked her arm angrily away. "How dare you!"

    "Look. My 'conglomerate' as you call it, is as much my baby as your store is your baby. Stop fighting me and let's talk about this like adults."

    "An adult, as you say, would not grab someone and force her around!"

    Alex felt himself begin to be swallowed by the dark flashing eyes. Fighting it, he snapped coldly, "You're right. My apologies." He made a stiff bow and stalked past her down the hall back to the living room.

    Olivia, bewildered, stood for a moment and collected her wits. It was time to go home.

She slipped into the front foyer, grabbed her coat, and was just about to sneak out the back kitchen door, when Dan came into the kitchen.

With just a momentary twinge of guilt she said, "Dan, I'm leaving. You'll be fine now. Give me a call tomorrow and tell me how it all ended."

"Olivia..."

Olivia put her finger on his lip. "Don't. I was happy to help. Just let me know how things went. Good night."

"I understand. Thanks for all your help tonight," he said, giving her a chaste kiss on the cheek. "And I didn't mean to upset you earlier this evening."

"I know."

Dan looked out the door at the snow. "Are you going to be okay driving home?"

"Absolutely. You know I'm intrepid. Nothing stops me. If anything does happen, I'll call you from my cell." She gave him a quick smile and a small wave then slipped out the door into what was now a real nor'easter. Head bent against the wind and snow, she made her way towards her car. Looking up briefly to get her bearings, her heart skipped a beat when she noticed a big black BMW parked near hers. With a shock she realized where she had seen Alex before. He was the man who had driven slowly by her store just as she was leaving. It all made sense.

Inside, Alex looked back over the crowd in the dining room only to find Olivia missing. Disgusted with himself for his soft-hearted musings and his need to see a face, a behavior he considered as out of place as Ogilvy's drunken behavior, Alex decided it was time to say good bye. He found Dan at the back kitchen door, just closing it against the blowing snow.

"Dan, it was a pleasure meeting you. Thank you for your hospitality. It's time for my uncle and I to take our leave," said Alex as he reached out to shake Dan's hand. "It was a pleasure meeting your girlfriend. Please let her know I said goodbye."

Dan hesitated a second while trying to decide whether to right Alex's incorrect impression of his relationship with Olivia. Quickly deciding it wouldn't do any harm to let it go, he simply said, "Olivia just left for home. She was exhausted from working all day. But, thank you. I'll let her know you thought of her."

With a curt nod, Alex went to collect his uncle. He found him sitting on the arm of the soft white sofa, slumped over a cornered Tiffany, whom he was regaling with drunken tales of jury trials he had fought as a young attorney. Alex took the bottle of Maker's Mark out of one of his hand and a rocks glass out of the other. "Hey! What do you think you're doing?"

"I think it's time for us to say good night. I've been traveling all day and would like to get some rest."

"Then you can go home like a good boy. I'm having a charming time with…with…what's your name young lady?" he slurred boozily into her face.

Tiffany pulled back and looked up to Alex with a beseeching look in her pale blue eyes.

"Sorry, Uncle. We only have one car and I've got the keys. We'll meet up with these folks another time. Here's your coat. Better put it on; it's pretty cold out there."

Barbier made a grab for his coat and fell forward over the arm of the sofa. Alex propped him up. "Come on. Everyone up. Let's go." Half carrying, half walking he propelled his protesting uncle out the door.

Olivia looked up from cleaning the snow off her car, as the front door opened. Slurred laughter of a man well beyond his limit came ringing out. The outdoor light shone down on the unmistakable figure of Alex Dumaurier supporting a sagging man as they lurched their way toward the car parked directly in front of hers. Quickly, she got into her car and prayed she hadn't been seen.

Alex, busy supporting Ogilvy, noticed a flash of movement by the cars, but the slipping man by his side took all his attention. Occupied stuffing Leo into his BMW, Alex did not look up at the old Volvo as it quietly inched by.

Chapter 3

Christmas morning dawned brilliant with winter sunlight. It shone through the lacy white curtains as Olivia, unable to sleep any longer, sat in bed under her Delft blue quilt, hugging a downy pillow to her chest. The jumbled events of the night before spun around her mind. Grudgingly, she admitted to herself that she had not felt such a visceral attraction to a man since the day she met Michael years ago in the café. Disloyally, the thought occurred to her that even then she had not felt this, this...this whatever it was. What was it? Just thinking about the stony planes of his face and his piercing grey eyes made her stomach dance. She was just going to have to ignore her traitorous body and focus on the battle ahead. A clear mind was what was needed here; not a schoolgirl's crush on a handsome face. She would need some information about him. Dan's boss was his uncle. Maybe Dan could find something out for her. Then she remembered Dan's nuzzling before the party and the confusion she had felt came rushing back.

Sighing, she got out of bed and went over to the window. Diaphanous white snow glittered in the sunlight and tree branches still held their hilly little coatings of snow, making the world appear innocent and fresh. It was hard to remain unsettled on such a beautiful morning. Olivia longed to be in it and decided to go for a good tromp through the woods before coming back and making herself a feast for breakfast.

Quickly, she changed from her pale yellow flannel pajamas into jeans and a warm navy blue sweater. She pulled on her tall winter boots, buttoned on an old olive green jacket, threw her colorful scarf around her neck, and settled her floppy-brimmed black hat over her ears.

Heading out to one of her favorite walks, she took the path that skirted the Meres mansion and then plunged into the woods of the state forest. Walking alongside the mansion she felt a possessive tenderness towards it, almost as though it were alive. Sadness filled her knowing that the history of this beautiful old house was slowly being lost each year as more and more of the ancient building decayed and frayed away. The absent owners of the estate had had it on the market for years, but no one had wanted to take on the responsibility of renovating and maintaining the old structure. She felt slightly guilty praying that no one would buy the old place; daydreaming about one day having enough money to buy the old mansion herself, putting in a cooking school, a vineyard, and growing an herb garden behind it big enough to supply the store. But then, that was a dream. For now, she simply enjoyed having it there; giving her a homey security in an odd sort of way.

When Olivia reached the entrance to the state forest, she was surprised to see the pristine snow marred by the footprints of a person with a dog.

Trying not to feel irritated, she told herself this person had as much right to enjoy this beautiful morning as she had. Nevertheless, she veered away from the main trail and decided to follow the deer track that skirted the pond a little way into the park.

The cold air invigorated her as her body warmed up from trekking through the unbroken snow. Olivia's spirits rose as the peace of the woods began to seep into her mind and infiltrate all parts of her body and soul. She was content.

Her peace was shattered by a huge black dog bounding through the brush heading straight for her. Olivia's heart jumped into her throat as the beast advanced on her without slowing, despite the snow. Abruptly, it came to a stop right in front of her and began to sniff her hands and legs as she stood stone still. She felt the mastiff's huge wet nose snuffling her jacket when inexplicably it leapt up, putting its enormous front paws on her shoulders. Olivia fought for balance, but the weight of the dog was too much. She flew backwards in a heap. The dog stood over her, for all the world looking like he was grinning, the massive paws pinning her down by the shoulders. Flailing in the deep cushion of snow, she desperately tried to push him away and right herself. Ridiculously, this only made the dog wag his broom of a tail even more happily and lick her face affectionately with a big wet tongue "Hey! Get off me you big mutt!"

A man's voice suddenly came ringing through the trees, "Buster! Come!" Again more loudly and insistently this time, "Buster! Come! Here, boy!"

The big dog's ears pricked up as the shouts came nearer. He bounded away joyfully only to come running back less than a minute later to find Olivia, now sitting up in the snow brushing herself off. Buster, or Olivia assumed it was Buster, plunked himself down next to her, his tongue lolling out of his mouth in delighted and contented panting.

"Sure. Ignore your master," she muttered looking at the panting dog. "Just look at what you've done to me. What kind of a master do you have anyway, who allows you to go around doing this to unsuspecting people? You could have hurt me…you know?" Olivia surveyed the huge face with the lolling tongue and large limpid black eyes fringed with vast shaggy eyebrows. "I guess you wouldn't intentionally hurt a fly, would you?" she asked, while rubbing him behind the ears. The insistent calling was very near now. Olivia looked up as a man crashed through the brush calling to the dog. Her jaw dropped as, unbelievably, she recognized the man as the abrasive owner of European Gourmet.

He stopped short. His shaggy dog, with a ridiculous grin on his panting face, lay innocently next to what appeared to be a snow-covered woman sitting in the snow. The droopy old hat hid the person's face, making it difficult to be sure the person was a woman. Quickly he ran to help, swearing under his breath.

He reached a hand out to pull her up. "I'm so sorry. Are you all right?" As Olivia rose, recognition dawned on his face. "You have got to be kidding me. What are you, of all people, doing here?"

"I may ask the same thing of you. I walk here all the time. This is the first time I've seen you here," she retorted angrily.

"Someone on my uncle's staff told me that this state forest was here, so here I am," he responded stiffly. "I didn't think there would be anyone else in the woods this morning, so I let Buster run off the leash. I'm afraid he's a little too friendly and enthusiastic sometimes, but he wouldn't hurt a fly …." His voice trailed away as he looked into Olivia's pink-cheeked face, her eyes still partially hidden under her floppy snow-covered hat.

"Are you sure nothing's broken? Here, let me help get some of this snow off." He reached to brush the snow off her hat brim and, softly, off her cheeks.

"I'm fine," she responded, her anger slipping away, "Just a little shaken."

Olivia peered at him from under the black felt hat. The sun glinted off his close-cropped brown hair and his eyes had lost their flintiness of the night before. Unexpected heat flowed through her, warming her in ways the tramp through the woods could not. Unexpectedly, he placed a gentle kiss on her cheek. Olivia felt like she was going to land in the snow again, this time from her treacherous knees deserting her when she needed them most.

Alex closed his eyes for a moment. "Damn!" he swore softly under his breath. He looked back at Olivia, the flint back in his eyes. "It appears that both Buster and I have lost our minds this morning. Believe me when I say I am not usually in the habit of assaulting women. Forgive me." Without giving her a chance to speak, he swung about, calling to Buster. The two of them disappeared into the brush as quickly as they had appeared, this time with Buster obeying at his heels.

Her peaceful morning shattered, Olivia headed back to her cottage, her mind reeling. How dare he? And why had she let him? As she stomped back home, she couldn't decide whether she was angrier with Alex or herself.

She wasn't hungry anymore, but decided to make herself breakfast anyway in the hopes of settling herself down and bringing some sense of normalcy to her life. Deliberately, she toasted a bagel and slathered it with cream cheese, then layered it with smoked salmon, paper-thin slices of red onions, fresh lemon juice, capers, and black pepper. She made herself a cappuccino with her little espresso maker, sank onto the chintz-cushioned window seat in front of the little oak table in the kitchen, and tried to coax back the feeling of tranquility she had found at the start of her walk. Still not hungry, she sat and hugged her knees to herself. Electric sparks still flew through her body just thinking of the kiss. Who was this baffling man? One minute she hated him because he was going to drive her out of business, the next minute she was practically swooning because he kissed her cheek in broad daylight!

Just then, her phone rang, making her jump two inches. She looked at the caller ID and recognized Dan's phone number. Her heart sank and she hesitated to answer. She didn't want to deal with Dan's need for her, nor did she want to talk to him about what just happened. She let it ring again, and then forced herself to answer.

"Hello?"

"Merry Christmas, Olivia! Isn't it a beautiful morning?" Dan's voice rang cheerily.

Olivia commanded herself to act like a normal friend. "It is beautiful out there. I've already been for a walk. Don't tell me you're just getting up, lazybones!" Involuntarily Olivia's thoughts traveled back to the image of Alex standing in front of her, gently lifting her hat away from her eyes. Immediately she squelched the memory and tried to focus on what Dan was saying.

"I thought you said you were going to laze in bed all day and do nothing?"

"I know, but it was too beautiful, I just had to get out."

"Olivia?" Silence.

"Yes?"

"About last night…"

"Forget about it Dan. We were both tired."

"I know, but I don't want to forget about it. We need to talk."

Olivia's heart sank. "I know Dan, but can we do it some other time?"

There was silence for a moment. Sadly, Dan replied, "Yes. Yes, I guess we can." There was silence for a few moments before Olivia asked, "Dan?"

"Yes."

"That guy who was at your party last night, Alex Dumaurier...do you know anything about him other than that he owns European Gourmet?"

"Nope. That was the first time I'd met him."

"Do you think there's any way you can find out what he's up to?"

"Mm...m...m...Maybe, maybe not. Leo is his uncle, but I don't know how much he'll tell me. If I hear of anything I'll let you know."

"Thanks. You're a great friend."

"Yeah, that's what I am...a great friend," he muttered to himself.

Olivia heard him, but chose to ignore it.

"I hope your party ended well."

"Jeez, Olivia! I'm sorry I didn't say something to you sooner. Thank you for all your help and for rescuing me!"

"No need to thank me. I just wanted to make sure everything ended up okay after all your worrying."

"It was great. Our new admin wanted me to tell you thank you for being so nice to her. I guess she didn't see you leave"

"Which person was that?"

"Do you remember Tiffany? She's really cute. She just started working at the firm a couple of weeks ago. Robert Morgan already has his talons on her and is the one who brought her to the party."

How could she have forgotten? "Now I remember. What possessed her to hook up with that guy? She seems like a nice enough girl, but I don't know about him."

"I think she was just flattered to be asked out by one of the lawyers. She's so new she really doesn't know anyone there yet. I suspect she is not going to do that again. She spent the rest of the evening staying as far away from him as possible. We actually had a really nice chat. She's a pretty smart kid!"

Olivia smiled. "Well, I'm glad it all turned out okay. Hey, Dan, I'm going to run off now. I feel like just vegging out and reading. I hope you don't mind. You'll let me know if you find out anything about Alex, won't you?"

"Sure. I understand. Get some rest. You deserve it." Dan promised to do what he could, then rang off.

Olivia spent the next day and a half sleeping, thinking, walking, and watching old movies. Finally, by Monday evening she began to feel rested and ready to take on the world again. Alex Dumaurier was not going to take over her life in any way, shape, or form!

Chapter 4

Alex marched out of the woods to his car parked down the road, angry with himself for acting like a teenager when it came to this woman. Opening the rear door, he commanded Buster to get in. Buster hopped into the back seat, turned around and gave him a reproachful look, then rested his head on his crossed paws. Alex ignored the look, got into the driver's seat, and sped off to his uncle's house. He felt like a fool.

Maybe the fact that he hadn't been with a woman in months had something to do with it. Sex was fine as recreation with no emotions attached, but a pounding heart was another thing entirely; something he wanted to avoid at all costs. History was not going to repeat itself.

He had married his parents' best friends' daughter Louise, right after graduating from Dartmouth. She had been young, silly, beautiful, and vivacious; someone he had lusted after and romantically thought would make life fun forever. Almost immediately after their elaborate wedding, Alex had gone to work in the family business. His grandparents had opened a pastry shop and prepared food business in Chicago soon after emigrating from France at the end of the Second World War. He had taken over at the helm when his father retired and was now making a name for himself in the industry with a business that was more successful than ever; opening several new locations each year.

Working long hours, he thought he had been building a wonderful future for his wife and the family he hoped to create with her. Then one day he had come home early from work to find her in bed with his best friend. Alex couldn't believe how blind he had been to what others had seen going on around him. His naïve heart had been shattered and he vowed never to let it happen again.

The divorce had been fast and Alex had poured all his hurt and pain into the building of an empire.

Chapter 5

Olivia went back to work at five thirty Tuesday morning, rested and reinvigorated. She always liked this time of day in the store when she felt a serene anticipation of what the day would bring - the proverbial calm before the storm. She walked through the front of the store turning on the lights and the soft classical music. While the first pot of coffee brewed, she went to look out the front windows at the snowy main street. The sky was just beginning to lighten, promising another sunny day. An occasional person carrying a briefcase hurried by to catch the early train to Manhattan. Everything was in its place.

Olivia poured herself an aromatic cup of coffee and walked into the kitchen to fire up the ovens. As she flipped on the switch to the exhaust fan, she heard a monstrous thunk, then a horrendous grinding and screeching. Quickly she flipped the switch off and looked under the hood to see what could possibly have happened. Nothing was immediately obvious. Mystified and worried since they had a heavy workload to prepare for New Year's at the end of the week, she called the emergency number on the exhaust hood that hung over the stovetop to try to get someone out right away to solve the problem.

The answering service voice indifferently replied that due to the holidays, it wouldn't be till late in the morning at the earliest before a serviceman could come out.

Luckily, Olivia thought, it was cold out and they could jury rig a system of fans and open windows until the repairmen showed up. Hopefully the health department would not decide to make a surprise visit today!

Harry walked in the back door to find Olivia dragging all the old floor fans up from the basement.

"Having a hot flash so early in the day?" he joked, wondering what on earth she was up to.

"Very funny. No, there's something terribly wrong with the exhaust fan and the repairmen can't get here till later on. We need to be able to blow the exhaust out the kitchen windows instead of letting it drift into the store. It's going to make the kitchen awfully cold, but we have to do it. Give me a hand will you?"

Together they brought all four huge fans up and set them strategically around the kitchen, blowing towards the wide open windows. Even the heat of the big ovens couldn't cut through the cold blowing in through the opening.

"Well, it's not perfect, but that should do it until we get things fixed." Olivia said gamely. They had too big a week ahead of them to let this slow them down. Today they had to clean up from Christmas, set up for New Years, and begin work on all the parties booked for that week. No time for moping about inconveniences. They would get through this, she promised herself... hopefully.

She looked over at Harry who was now standing staring off into space, his hands gripping his first cup of coffee, looking pensive. "What are you thinking about?" she asked.

"Do you remember Tommy from Jake's restaurant?"

"Yes. How could I forget? I thought you two were going to be together for life. Though honestly, I didn't think he treated you as well as you deserved. Why?"

"I bumped into him on Christmas Eve, when I was at the bar with John. He kind of went crazy on me, saying that I was a two-timing double crosser and a lot more. Said he was going to get even with me when I least expected it. You know, *he's* the one who broke up with me. I felt like a jerk in front of John. We got out of there as fast as we could. He gave me the creeps. I can't believe I ever liked him."

"How awful. What did John think?"

"He was actually great about it. I don't know why it's upsetting me so much now. John and I actually had a great weekend together. He's a really nice guy. Even you might approve."

Olivia smiled. "We'll just have to see about that. You'll have to bring him by so I can check him out."

"Maybe I'll wait a little before doing that. Your checking him out is more like an interrogation."

"Am I really that bad? It's just because I care about you, and you must admit you don't have a great track record."

"Yeah, I know. Oh well. Let me get cranking here." With a sigh, he walked over to the coffee bar to begin the morning set-up.

The back door opened and merry chatter could be heard as Lena, Olivia's sous chef Gilberta, and the rest of the staff drifted in to work.

"What the hell happened?" demanded Gilberta as she rounded the corner and surveyed the fans and open windows.

"And good morning to you, too," responded Olivia. Gilberta was not one to mince words.

Gilberta gave a wry grin. "Yeah. It doesn't look like a good morning, but good morning. So, what happened?"

"The exhaust fan is broken, so I rigged a system to keep the exhaust out of the store." Olivia filled everyone in on the morning's events. Gilberta looked around and shrugged her shoulders.

"A woman's got to do, what a woman's got to do." With good grace, she skirted the floor fans and cords, tied an apron on over her parka and got to work. The others looked uncertain, but soon followed suit.

Around noon, Olivia's bookkeeper Diane entered the kitchen with an envelope in her hand. Olivia was standing by the stove straining a red wine sauce she had just finished. "Hey, Olivia, here's a notice from your landlord. When does your lease end with him?"

"Five years are up at the end of April. It's probably time to renegotiate. Why? What does he say?"

"Looks like he is trying to raise the rent twenty-five percent. Can he do that?"

Olivia looked at Diane in horror. "Twenty-five percent? I don't remember if legally he can. I'll give him a call and see what's going on. He must think I'm made of gold. I can't believe he's trying to do that in this economy!"

"It is amazing, considering what a great tenant you have been. I can't imagine him being able to get anyone more reliable. Well, I'll put this letter on your desk for you to look at later, then," said Diane sympathetically as she walked out of the kitchen.

Olivia worried for a moment about what would happen if her already high rent were to go up a full twenty-five percent. However, she had work to do; the lease was good till April and now was not the time to focus on the issue. When this week was over, she was going to review the lease again to remind herself of what it said. She was pretty sure the landlord was allowed only a cost of living increase, and not this outrageous arbitrary number. Dan had helped her with the original lease. She would give him a call later.

Gilberta looked over as Olivia finished straining the sauce. "My grandmother used to say bad things come in threes. Here's number two. I wonder what's next."

"Gilberta! That's just an old superstition. Anyway, I'll probably be able to negotiate a reasonable lease, so this is not necessarily a bad thing. Just something you have to deal with as a business owner."

"We'll see."

Olivia shook her head in exasperation and went on with her work. Gilberta was a wonderful cook and hard worker, but the superstitions she had learned from her grandmother were something else. Every time someone spilled salt or pepper, she warned that something bad was going to happen. If someone's apron fell off, she would tease them that their sweetheart was thinking of them. She could go on endlessly. Most of the time it was amusing; today, she didn't feel like hearing it.

Two burly repairmen arrived late in the day, just as the store was closing. They found Olivia in the kitchen putting away filet mignon she had just finished marinating for one of tomorrow's parties. Relieved finally to have them there after thinking they were not going to show up, she gave them a quick report on what she had heard that morning. They examined the interior of the hood and not finding anything inside, went to the roof to see what they could find from the other end.

Snow covered, they came back down a few minutes later with quizzical looks on their faces. One of them carried a heavy boulder in his arms. "Well, this is a first. I think someone threw this down your vent, and I don't think it came from Santa Claus. This was no accident," said the man. "There's no way this got in there on its own. You piss someone off?"

Bewildered, Olivia shook her head, "Not that I know of. What kind of damage did it do? Can you fix it?"

"Lady, it pretty much wrecked the whole fan system in there. I hate to say it, but you're gonna have to put in a whole new fan and motor."

Olivia's stomach clenched. Steeling herself she asked, "Ok, tell me how long it will take you to get the parts and repair it, and do we have to close the kitchen while you work?"

"We probably can get the parts tomorrow. All of the work can be done from the roof, so if we don't get a blizzard, we can probably get it all done tomorrow without you shutting the kitchen down. But it's gonna cost you. We need a thousand dollar deposit to start and then whatever the balance is will have to be paid tomorrow when we finish."

Olivia tried not to think about the money. "Ok, do what you have to do. Do you have a ball park idea of the total cost?"

Harry groaned loudly as he stepped into the kitchen and overheard the repairman tell Olivia the total cost of the repairs. "Good thing we had a good holiday season, isn't it?" he said wryly to Olivia as she headed downstairs to make out a check for the deposit.

Olivia thoughtfully watched the repairmen leave out the back door. It occurred to her that it might be smart to call the police to have them look at the boulder and let them know what happened. She would put the beef away and then call.

Gilberta, noticing Olivia's distraction, came over and took the sheet pan out of her hands. "Go do what you have to do and I'll take care of this."

Gratefully, Olivia handed over her work. "Thank you," she smiled wanly before leaving the kitchen. Downstairs, she paused as she lifted the phone. *Who would want to destroy her business more than European Gourmet? Was Alex capable of this?*

A trim businesslike policewoman arrived within ten minutes. She took notes while Olivia answered her questions. "It's possible this is just a bad prank by local kids, but just to cover all the bases, do you know of anyone who would want to hurt you or the store, such as employees you might have fired?"

Olivia wracked her brain but could think of no employees who had left on bad terms, nor anyone who might want to cause trouble for her. And then the thought of Alex Dumaurier and European Gourmet crossed her mind again. No....That was impossible. Or was it?

"I really can't think of anyone who has worked here who would want to hurt me or the store," she said. Then hesitatingly, she added, "There is only one person I can think of right now who might wish this business did not exist. The CEO for

European Gourmet is in town. I believe European Gourmet is considering putting a store in the area, but I can't imagine in my wildest dreams that they would do something like this."

"Well, that's worth checking out, even if it doesn't turn anything up. You never know." said the policewoman.

Olivia felt like a traitor giving the policewoman what little information she knew about Alex. In her mind's eye, she saw him dressed in his jeans and snow boots, and it just did not seem possible that he could be involved with something as petty and mean as throwing a rock down a vent. And then there was the kiss.

"Did the repairmen happen to notice any footprints up there, do you know?" asked the policewoman, bringing her out of her reverie.

"They didn't mention any, and I was too stunned at the time to think about asking them whether they had or not," replied Olivia "I have their phone number and they are coming back tomorrow if you want to talk to them."

"I think I'll stop by tomorrow. Who knows, I might be able to pick up a little more information. Meanwhile, let me know if you remember anything else. It's a shame this had to happen to you at this time of year," she said shaking her head sympathetically as she left to file her report.

Olivia turned around to find her kitchen staff looking at her in astonishment.

"I can't believe anybody would do something like that! A boulder down the vent?" exclaimed Gilberta disgustedly. "We're just a small food store, for Pete's sake! Why would anyone bother to hurt us?"

Olivia shook her head slowly, "I don't understand it either, but I'm going to try not to let it get me down. Hopefully, the police will come up with an answer. Anyway, we can't do anything about it at the moment, so let's try to forget it and just concentrate on finishing up what we're doing."

They all turned back to their tasks of chopping, grilling, and sautéing for the mountain of orders already placed. The store hummed busily with sounds of coffee being ground, shelves being restocked, registers ringing, knives chopping, and mixers whirring. Subdued chatter went on around Olivia as she concentrated on the chocolate mousse cakes she was glazing with rich, shiny chocolate ganache. Usually the sounds were a soothing symphony to her ears, but now they could not soothe away the knot in her stomach and the strong sense of foreboding she felt.

Chapter 6

When she finally got home that night, she found the message light blinking on the answering machine. After putting her chef's coat in the washing machine and pouring herself a glass of Pinot Noir, she walked over and pushed the button to listen to the message.

It was Dan. "Hi Olivia. I didn't want to bother you at work. I have some info you might be interested in on Alex Dumaurier. The biggest news is that he put a deposit on the Meres mansion. Give me a call when you get a chance. I'll be up late so don't worry about calling when you get home. Bye."

Olivia's knees felt like they were going to buckle underneath her. Her world was beginning to tumble around her ears.

Bleakly, she picked up the phone and dialed Dan's number. Dan picked up on the first ring.

"Oh Dan," she choked, "The mansion! What's he planning on doing with it?"

"Don't know," he replied. "It's not zoned for commercial use so he can't put a store there, unless he goes before Planning and Zoning to petition for a change of zoning. So one of the most logical things he could do would be to tear it down, subdivide the lot and build several houses for resale. Another option would be to renovate the mansion itself into many apartments or condos and rent or sell them that way. But I don't really know what he's planning. Who knows? Maybe he's planning on living in it."

Olivia remained silent for a long time, trying to absorb the implications of these possibilities. Maybe Gilberta's grandmother was right, after all. This was the third disaster in one day!

"Olivia? Are you ok?" asked Dan in a concerned voice.

"I don't know if I'm ok, but I'm still breathing. Dan, you won't believe this, but something else happened today, too. Someone threw a large rock down the kitchen vent sometime between Christmas Eve and this morning when I came to work, totally wrecking the fan and motor."

"What! Oh, Olivia! I'm so sorry! Can you keep working? Is there anything I can do to help?"

"Well, I've got the police looking for who did it and the repairmen say they probably can get it fixed tomorrow for a pretty sum, so I don't need that kind of help," replied Olivia. "But Dan, is it just coincidence that Alex Dumaurier seems to be around all the things that are happening right now? I feel like my world is falling apart and it all started when he came to town. I know I'm probably overreacting, but I saw his car cruising slowly by the store several times Christmas Eve. What if he's the one who threw the rock down the vent? I'm worried about the store being blown up, and on top of that, my beautiful mansion might be torn down and replaced by a bunch of those horrible Mcmansions!"

"Whoa! Let's take things one at a time," soothed Dan. "Just because his car went by your store doesn't mean he wants to destroy you; and I'm pretty certain he's not the kind of person who would do something as small minded as throwing a rock down a vent. And we don't know what he's planning for the mansion, so it's useless to worry about that right now."

"You're probably right," sighed Olivia. "But Dan, I did tell the policewoman about him and she's probably going to look into it."

"That's fine. You did what you had to do. I expect nothing will come of it except maybe Alex getting peeved. You know Olivia, he's not a bad guy. You might even like him if you gave yourself the chance to get to know him. I talked with him for quite a while today. He *is* interested in the town as a location for a new store, which is something you need to be concerned about, but other than that he's seems like a reasonable fellow."

"He may be a reasonable guy, but he's encroaching on my territory and I'm certainly not happy about what he could do with the Meres mansion."

"Olivia, your concerns are totally legitimate, but things may work out better than you think. Try not to worry so much unless something concrete happens. If I hear of anything that could harm you I will let you know, and… if I can, try to put an end to it," he added trying to reassure her.

"Thanks for keeping me sane, Dan. Meanwhile, I'm going to try to get through this week with flying colors. If my clients are happy, they won't need to go to anyone else," she said more steadily now. "I'll let you know if we find out anything about that rock and who dropped it down the vent. I guess I'll talk to you tomorrow."

"Alright. Try to get some sleep. Good night, Olivia."

Olivia was just about to hang up when she remembered the letter from the landlord. "Dan! You still there?"

"I'm here. What's up?" replied Dan bringing the receiver back to his ear.

"I just remembered that I received a letter from Hotchkiss today. Remember he's my landlord? He wants to raise the rent by twenty-five percent in April when the old lease is up. I think I'm going to need help renegotiating the new lease. Can you help?"

"Sure. I'll take a look at the copy in my office when I get a chance."

"I really can't think of this until after New Year's Eve," said Olivia tiredly.

"No worries. It'll wait. Meanwhile get some sleep, if you can."

"Yes sir. Goodnight," smiled Olivia hanging up. Dan truly was a wonderfully dear person. Maybe he was the right one for her, after all. If only she felt that spark she had felt with Michael. But, perhaps that kind of love only came once in a lifetime and this love could be just as fulfilling. She certainly felt a need for him right now.

Though Dan had made her feel somewhat better, Olivia still felt an emptiness and despair she hadn't felt in a long time. Michael had been the center of her universe and the plane crash that had wrenched him away from her just a month before they were to be married had left a gaping hole in her life that had just begun to heal. It felt like the hole was being torn open again.

Chapter 7

The crisp sunny weather held up for another day and Olivia's spirits rose as masses of customers swarmed through her store. Smiling, she headed to the back door with Gilberta, her chef coat sleeves rolled up, ready to help load the catering equipment into the truck for that evening's event. She grabbed a crate of equipment, only to hear a large serving fork that had not been properly wrapped into the kit clang to the floor. Gilberta immediately sang out, "Ooh, you're going to get a visit from a man!"

"Gilberta...how can my dropping a fork mean that a man is going to visit?" Olivia sighed, stooping down to pick up the offending item.

Gilberta stopped what she was doing and looked meaningfully behind Olivia. Olivia stood up and turned around to come face to face with a stony Alex Dumaurier, looking commanding and distinguished in a well-cut black suit and crisp white shirt, the point of a white silk handkerchief neatly showing in his lapel pocket. Harry stood behind him with a distressed look on his face, silently mouthing, "Sorry. I couldn't stop him."

"Ms. Caron, may I speak with you a moment?" Alex asked in an icy voice, oblivious to the angst he was causing Harry.

The unwanted memory of his kiss in the woods sent shivers through her. She forced herself to look up into his eyes and received a piercingly cold look in return. All thoughts of kisses quickly evaporated.

Taking a deep breath, she looked over Alex's shoulder and said, "It's ok, Harry. I'll take care of this."

"I'll be by the register if you need me," he said with a meaningfully look at Olivia and then disappeared back to the front of the store.

Olivia focused on Alex, trying to read his inscrutable eyes. It occurred to her that this was not the type of man to drop a boulder down a vent; no, he would do something much more subtle and devastating. She felt incredibly brainless for having even thought it could be possible, still she was not sorry she told the police about him. "Are you here to gloat?" she asked sarcastically.

"I'm assuming you are talking about your fan incident. Contrary to what you may think, I am not here to gloat. I do want a mystery cleared up, though. Why did you tell the police you thought I might have something to do with it?"

Gilberta, who had been gawking in the background, watched as a wave of pink washed into Olivia's cheeks. She reached for the fork in Olivia's hands and shooed her off. "Go take care of this, Olivia. I have the party under control."

Olivia glared at her, then took off her apron and smoothed the tendrils of hair that had gotten loose from her scarf, fully aware of how untidy she must look. Struggling to gain control, she turned back to Alex. Stiffly she said, "Let's get out of the way." She glanced to the front of the store and noticed the empty coffee bar seats. "I could use some coffee. Would you like a cup?"

Alex looked at this appealing and disheveled woman. The venom he had felt earlier that morning when being questioned by the police began to melt away. "A cup of coffee would be welcome, thank you."

Olivia led Alex over to the coffee bar. She felt his presence next to her, but dared not look over. Silently, they poured their coffees, then walked over and sat down at the warm wooden hi-top table in the bay window that overlooked the bustling main street. Olivia sipped her coffee, wrapping her hands tightly around her cup, avoiding Alex's eyes.

"Though I don't appreciate being grilled by the police, my real reason for being here is curiosity. What made you think I could be involved in this matter?" asked Alex.

Feeling foolish for having thought for one minute this tough businessman could stoop to petty destruction, Olivia's cheeks reddened even further. She forced herself to look up into his eyes.

"I saw your car crawling back and forth in front of my store Christmas Eve. That was the only strange thing that I'd seen happen around here, so I told the policewoman about it," she admitted, wishing she didn't sound like a defensive schoolgirl.

Alex's eyebrows raised in surprise. So, she had seen him. "Fair enough. I suppose I might have done the same thing, if I were in your shoes."

"Why were you driving by my store, Mr. Dumaurier? What does it have to do with your business?"

"My company *is* exploring this town as a possible site for a new store. I was told by my staff that you had a delightful business here that warranted being looked at."

"I don't believe there is room for two such similar stores in this town, Mr. Dumaurier."

"Please, call me Alex. You may be right, but strategically for us, it fits into the triangle of stores we plan on building in Connecticut. This town has the perfect location for the central store in the state."

Olivia stared down at the coffee cup she held in her hands, avoiding his eyes, as she took in the enormity of what he was saying. Breathing did not seem to be on the list of possibilities.

She swallowed hard. Damn it! She would simply have to come up with something creative in order to survive, because she was going to survive. No, more than that, she was going to thrive!

Resolute, she lifted her eyes and looked directly into his. "Do what you must do Mr. Dumaurier, but let me warn you....I will not be put out of business."

Alex returned the look - and dove helplessly into the flashing depths of the dark eyes. A shiver ran through him. This woman had the power to touch those long-locked emotions hidden deep inside. What he wouldn't give to have her in his arms, devouring those lips he had had no right to kiss in the first place. Alex gave himself a mental shake and surfaced. "Ms. Caron, I simply wish to continue growing my business and this town represents the logical next step. Couple that with the collapsed price of real estate, and one finds that now is the right time."

"I understand wanting to grow your business, though how you go about it is another matter entirely," she replied curtly.

"I assure you I would not think to destroy competition in such a criminal manner as this. Fair competition is one thing; physically damaging a business is another."

Olivia studied him over her cup of coffee. She believed him. But, he still potentially held the power to totally destroy her world. Somehow, she would find the way not to hand that power over to him.

"Mr. Dumaurier, may I be nosy and ask another totally unrelated question, which really is none of my business?"

He raised an eyebrow, wondering what in the world could be coming next. "Please, call me Alex; and yes, by all means, ask your question."

"Alright…Alex. What are you planning on doing with the Meres mansion?"

Alex was totally taken aback; but then he remembered…she was Dan's girlfriend, wasn't she? And Dan worked for his uncle. So why shouldn't she know about his interest in the property? Dan probably talked to her about everything. He made a note to himself to watch what he said around him. He'd have to talk to his uncle about that, as well.

"At the moment I have no concrete plans. My staff has determined that it is an attractive investment. Why? Does it interest you?"

"I bought the little stone caretaker's cottage just down the road from it a year ago and fell in love with the old mansion," she admitted. "I would really hate to see it disappear. I was wondering if I could convince you to renovate it rather than tear it down."

Alex's eyes softened imperceptibly as he looked at this unexpected woman in her baggy chef's coat, her fingers tightly gripping her coffee cup. "I am not bulldozing it down today, Ms. Caron, rest assured." How was it possible she owned the property next to the one he was considering? Was fate playing a joke on him?

Just then two workmen approached the table. "Ms. Caron, we finished putting in the new fan and motor. Works like a charm. Can you just sign these papers? And we need to get a check from you for the balance, three thousand four hundred and fifty dollars."

Alex glanced at Olivia as she sighed. "Give me a minute, guys. Grab a cup of coffee and something to eat and I'll be right with you."

"Sure thing," they said as they walked towards the bakery.

"I have to get going," said Olivia rising from her seat. Her stomach betrayed her and did its lightning dance again as Alex took her hand in both of his.

"I wish you the best of luck Ms. Caron, and I am truly sorry your equipment was damaged. Perhaps we'll see each other in the woods again, though next time I will keep Buster on his leash!"

With a nod, he was gone, and Olivia stood alone, her heart pounding wildly.

Chapter 8

New Year's Eve arrived with ten cocktail parties to send out in ten different directions. She had hired extra trucks, brought on a bartending service to add to her team, and called in all staff. Men and women in tuxedos bumped into each other in the loading area, focused on loading trucks with food and equipment; party captains read their party sheets for special instructions; and party chefs reviewed their menus. Olivia buzzed from one group to the next making sure every little detail was being attended to and nothing left behind. Finally, the last party drove off to its destination and Olivia sat alone at her desk in her tiny office in the basement.

Footsteps could be heard over her head, and the store still sounded quite busy. Just as she was about to go upstairs to help, she heard a crash, then the confused commotion of footsteps and someone running down the stairs. Harry appeared in the office doorway, ghostly pale and breathless.

"Olivia, you'll never believe this! Someone threw a rock through one of the front windows, and it's totally smashed! Come upstairs…quick!"

Light-headed and weak-kneed Olivia followed Harry up the stairs at a run. Gilberta's warning about bad things coming in threes rang in her ears. Surely this was more than three!

"Is anybody hurt?"

"No, luckily no one was sitting at the coffee bar. Everyone was pretty much at the registers checking out. It was just scary!"

"Did anybody see anyone?"

"No, we were all busy helping customers when it just happened!"

"Go call the police while I look around," Olivia ordered.

A few customers were milling around curiously talking amongst themselves. Olivia went to the gaping window to see if she could find what had come through and shattered it. Amongst the shards of glass under the coffee bar lay a fist-sized stone.

Quietly, she asked the customers to leave the area and placed chairs around the broken glass, preventing anyone from stepping on it.

In no time, Harry came up to her, the police in tow. "Hey, Olivia, want me to close up?"

Numbly, Olivia focused on Harry, trying to think logically. "Thanks, Harry. That would be great. Could you also call the Mancarella Glass Company down the road to see if they'd be willing to make an emergency stop on New Year's Eve. Maybe, if we're lucky, we can get something put in tonight, even if it's temporary. If not, I don't know what we're going to do."

The policewoman, who had been in earlier in the week, now waited with another sober young police officer while Olivia made the arrangements.

"This doesn't seem to be your week," she said ironically. "We haven't found any leads to your first problem yet and now this. I'm going to assume the two incidences are somehow connected. Can you tell me anything about what happened?"

Olivia recounted Harry's story, then showed them the rock she had found under the table. Again, for the second time in a week, she tried thinking of who could possibly want to harm her. Again, she came up with a blank.

The two police officers finished looking over the window. "We need to take the stone to the lab. It's highly unlikely we'll find anything on it, but you never know. We'll be in touch about that. Meanwhile, we're going to patrol your store through the night to make sure nothing else happens," said the policewoman.

"Thanks. I really appreciate it." She handed the two officers a bag of chocolate chunk cookies and sent them to help themselves to cups of coffee to get them through their shift.

Harry was just putting the phone down when Olivia walked behind the food counter. "I got hold of the glass people. Luckily, you made some emergency cake for the guy's daughter, so he's really grateful and said he would come over and see what he can do. He didn't promise anything, though. That's a big piece of glass, and he thinks he's going to have to special order it."

"Great. Let's hope he can do something. If he can't we'll have to find a tarp and some wood just to cover it. What a way to end the holidays!" Slowly, she walked around the store. Despite Harry and her staff, she felt bereft, helpless, and alone. She needed a friend – a shoulder to cry on right about now. Slowly, she walked down to her office.

Closing the door behind her, Olivia pressed Dan's number.

Her voice at once put him on the alert. "What's wrong?"

"Dan, someone just threw a rock through the front window of the store. It's completely shattered. Sounds like a bad mystery novel, doesn't it? I just can't believe this is happening again."

Dan whistled softly through his teeth. "Wow. Have you called the police?"

"Yes. They just left," she sighed. "They took the stone back to the lab with them. I must admit, I would feel a lot better if you were here."

"I'll be right there. I was just about to leave anyway. Don't let Harry leave until I get there. OK?"

"OK. Thanks, Dan." Slowly she opened the office door and headed back upstairs.

Fifteen minutes later Dan walked through the back door just as the glass company arrived. He took a look around while Olivia went over to talk to the repairmen.

One of the men, looking grizzled and tired after a long day, shook Olivia's hand, "I'm Gus Mancarella. You made a fantastic cake for my daughter. I don't know if you remember, but her baby was being christened and her friend was supposed to have made the cake. Of course, wouldn't you know it, her friend backed out at the last minute.

She called you, and even though you were busy, you made a cake for her, and boy, it was the most beautiful cake she'd ever seen. It tasted pretty good, too. I think I had three pieces, but don't tell her that!" he laughed. Looking at the front window, his face turned serious. "Now, what can I do for you? I see you have a broken window."

"I'm very grateful you came over on such short notice, Mr. Mancarella. Someone threw a rock through the front window and I have to do something about it tonight, but I don't know what's possible."

"Holy crow, will you look at that!" exclaimed another of the sturdy workmen who had gone to the front of the store. "Who in their right mind would do such a thing on New Year's Eve? At least they could have waited till Monday!"

"Well, let's take a look. We certainly can't let it blow open all weekend. Give me a few minutes to figure this out. We'll see what we can do."

Grateful and relieved, Olivia left them to measure the window while she helped close registers. The routine work calmed her shattered nerves and gave her a sense of normalcy.

Dan and Harry had cleaned up most of the glass when the fatherly repairman came up to Olivia. "Well…it's what I was afraid of. We don't have a big enough piece of glass that's strong enough to do the job in the shop right now, and we won't be able to get it till Monday. But, I'll tell you what, I'll send one of the boys back for some sheets of plywood and we'll board it up, so at least you'll be safe, and no one can come in to steal anything. How's that?"

Olivia smiled weakly. "That would be wonderful. Thank you so much for helping. I hope I didn't ruin any plans you might've had to go out tonight?"

"Honey, my only plans are to sit in my big chair in front of the TV, put my slippers on, and watch a good movie with the wife. Let the young kids party tonight. Me, I like it at home."

Olivia smiled wistfully as he left, thinking that that sounded perfect indeed. But, for the moment, she had a business she loved that needed some care. Other dreams would have to wait. She walked into the kitchen to see if everything was properly closed up. Satisfied, she came out with a thoughtful expression on her face. Harry, having closed down the front, looked at her somber face. "Are you okay?" he asked.

"Yes, but I wonder if the crews coming back tonight will be safe unloading. It almost seems like we should have someone here, just to make sure. I know the police will be patrolling, but I'd hate for anything to happen to the staff after a hard night. I think I'll come back just to make sure everything is alright."

Harry didn't hesitate. "I don't have any big plans for tonight. John's away and you know how I hate New Year's Eve. What if I come back around one to help unload the parties coming in? I might even call a cop to come over and keep me company.

That way you can get some rest. You're going to need it."

Olivia looked at Harry gratefully. "Thank you, Harry. I think that's a great idea. I can't believe you're volunteering to do it, but I'll accept your offer."

Dan, coming back from helping the window crew put in the plywood window, looked at Olivia thoughtfully. "I don't know if I like the idea of you staying in your house alone tonight. Why don't you sleep over my house?"

"Dan, I'll be fine. I'll keep my cell phone by me all the time, in case I need to call the police, but no one has come near the house. Don't you have your own plans for tonight?"

"No. Last week's party was enough excitement for me. I'm staying home."

"Well, why don't you and Harry come to my house for dinner? It's the least I can do, for all your help. I'll even let you check whether anyone's hiding in the closets. And, Harry, you can take a nap in my guest room after dinner. I'll wake you up in time to come back here at one. What do you say?" she asked looking at the two of them.

"Deal," said Dan

"Sounds like a plan," said Harry.

Chapter 9

New Year's Day arrived bleak and glacial. Last night had ended calmly and uneventfully, with Dan going home after a cozy dinner reminiscing about the first days of the business. Harry had taken a nap and then had gone to see the crews in, before heading to his own home.

Looking out her living room window at the grey sky, Olivia's anxiety got the better of her and she decided to drive over to the store to make sure nothing more had happened.

Though the heat was on in the store, her breath still came out in little white puffs. The wounded window let in much of the cold air.

She went downstairs to the office to read the party notes left by the returning catering staff. She smiled and sighed in relief. The staff was top notch, but she never rested easy until she had read the reports. All the parties had gone splendidly. Mrs. Dupont had even asked about scheduling another event at the end of January. At least business was something she didn't need to worry about.

Olivia walked back upstairs and was about to lock the store up when she heard a firm rapping on the back kitchen window. She looked over and saw Alex, dressed in the old jeans and parka he had been wearing that day in the woods, peering in. She froze. This was the last person she wanted to see right now. Alex rapped on the window again, catching her eye and signally her to come over. Thawing a little, she walked slowly towards the window; stopping just close enough to hear him speak through the glass.

"Olivia, I was just driving by and saw the plywood up front," he shouted through the window. "What happened?"

Olivia sighed to herself, then decided to go out and speak to Alex civilly, rather than scream through the window. She wrapped her coat tightly against the cold, and walked out the back door to where he stood, Buster by his side.

She looked stonily at him, "You really don't know?"

"No, I really don't know. Why? Should I?"

She studied him closely, but could detect nothing other than a questioning look. "Someone's been reading too many mystery novels and decided to send a rock through the front window," she explained wryly.

Alex looked truly stunned. "Olivia, I'm sorry." Suddenly he scowled and his flinty eyes scoured her face. "You don't really think I had anything to do with this again, do you?"

"I don't trust anybody right now," she replied bleakly. Buster, ignoring the tension, sniffed her affectionately. She knelt down and gave him a rub behind his ears. He immediately gave her a big wet lick on the cheek. Olivia felt her mood thaw a bit more and hugged the shaggy head.

Alex watched her rub his dog's ears, feeling ridiculously jealous. He ignored that thought. "I can only reassure you I had nothing to do with this," he said quietly. Olivia ignored the comment, studiously focusing on Buster's right ear. "Look, can we go somewhere warm to talk? It's a little chilly out here."

Olivia gave him an assessing look, while her traitorous stomach still managed butterflies. The grey eyes appeared to hold nothing but sincerity. She stood up. "Why should I trust you?"

Alex gripped her shoulders hard, looking straight into her eyes. "Because you can."

Olivia looked at this intense man and knew he had nothing to do with the window. He represented a bigger threat. Could she convince him to open his store in another town? At the moment, he seemed like a reasonable person. "We can't bring Buster into the store; as you know, it's against health codes. Anyway, the store is almost as cold as the outside right now." She paused, then said, "All the shops are closed. If you want, we can go to my house for a cup of coffee."

"I accept the offer."

"Give me a minute to finish up here, then we can go," she replied. "I'll be right back." Olivia went back in and finished locking up, all the while wondering if she was a fool. She walked back out, closing the door tightly behind her. "Do you know how to get there?" she asked.

"Pretty much. I've been to Meres to take a look at it. You're just down the road, right?"

"Yes, but why don't you follow me in your car? That way you won't get lost."

"Lead on. I'll be right behind."

Olivia climbed into her car and waited for the black BMW to pull out of its space. A short while later they were sitting at the heavy old oak table in Olivia's kitchen. The golden glow of the lamp hanging from the ceiling softened the cold grey light infiltrating through the mullioned windows. Buster lay contentedly at Olivia's feet gnawing on a chew toy Alex had given him.

Alex looked around the kitchen, which smelled of cinnamon and vanilla, thinking how well it suited Olivia. The pale apricot walls behind the unusual ancient black Aga range made the room elegantly cozy, while the thick butcher-block counters, worn smooth from years of use, evoked a sense of timelessness. There was a simple honesty and beauty in that old room that made him yearn to stay forever.

An uncomfortable silence surrounded them as they drank their coffee.

It was Olivia broke the stillness first. "As I said before, I don't trust anyone right now… and especially not you. I'm not saying you did the damage to my store, but you are looking to put a business in town which has the potential to put me out of business. You also are thinking of buying my mansion…I mean the Meres mansion, which is worrisome; though compared to losing my store, it's a small worry."

Alex remained quiet. His success had not come by allowing emotions to rule over objectivity and rationality. If anything, Olivia was being more rational than he was. He looked at her steadily, still fighting against the attraction he did not want to acknowledge. Somehow, this woman had worked her way well under his skin in a very short period of time. Curtly he said, "I can appreciate your thoughts."

Olivia forced herself to look squarely into the eyes of this man sitting across from her in her old wooden armchair. One moment he looked like he belonged in a boardroom, the next he looked more comfortable hanging out with Paul Bunyan in a lumberjack camp. At the moment, he looked nothing like the ruthless businessman she had first met. The carelessly rolled up sleeves of his flannel shirt revealed sinewy arms obviously used to working hard, and his long legs, with the worn jeans conforming to the tight muscles in his thighs, looked like they had hiked many a trail. His chin was covered with day-old stubble that held a touch of grey, which, if truth be told, gave him an appealingly roguish air, and his usually stern mouth now looked somewhat softer and more inviting. The kiss in the snow came back to haunt her. She was a fool for inviting him into her home.

Alex returned her gaze unflinchingly.

Quickly, she tore her eyes away from him. What was she thinking? On one hand, she didn't trust him in the least, on the other she was dreaming about what his lips would feel like on her own. Olivia felt like she was losing her grip on all normal behavior. Her world was tumbling into a bad telenovela.

Maddeningly, her heart gave a wild thump as Alex straightened up suddenly and took hold of her hands. He gripped them tightly and said, "Listen. I don't want to hurt you, directly or indirectly. Maybe there's some way we can work together, as opposed to fighting each other." He drew her hands to his lips and softly kissed them.

Her eyebrows flew up and her heart raced wildly as she felt her insides melting against her will. Thoughts of threats slid out of her mind as that small gesture sent shoots of electricity zinging through her. Dammit! Angrily, she stood up, attempting to yank her hands out of his.

Silently, Alex rose along with her, refusing to let go. Releasing one hand, he cupped the curls behind her ears and firmly drew her towards him.

Shocked, Olivia remained stone still as his lips, gentle and caressing, brushed softly against hers. A ridiculous rush of desire overwhelmed her. His gentleness dissolved into demanding fire as the kiss deepened, spun, and intensified, fueled by a yearning neither willingly yielded to. Nothing else existed; nothing else mattered. For that moment.

Abruptly, with a ragged breath, Alex let go. Olivia drew away, slowly coming back to reality. Too stunned to say anything, they both just stood there, staring at each other.

Alex whispered hoarsely. "I won't be responsible for my actions if I stay here any longer. I should go."

"Yes," responded Olivia weakly. "Go."

Silently, Alex put his coat on and grabbed Buster's leash. Looking back at Olivia as he headed out the door he spoke. "I have to go to Chicago for a while. Let's talk about our businesses when I get back."

"I'm not sure what business we have to talk about," Olivia managed to answer.

Chapter 10

The police called later that afternoon. Implausibly, they had been able to get a fingerprint off the stone, but, unfortunately, there was no match in any of the files. They had scheduled intermittent patrols to go by her store throughout the day, as well as her home. If anything new came up, they would call.

Olivia put down the phone. It was nice to know someone was keeping an eye on her. Keeping an eye on her…maybe she needed to keep an eye on herself. She put her fingers to her lips and felt Alex's kiss still lingering on her lips. She closed her eyes, remembering the voltage that had coursed between them. Not even her beloved Michael had sparked such a fierce reaction.

The phone rang again. This time it was Dan. Olivia looked at the phone as it rang insistently, then finally answered it.

"Hey, want to go out to dinner with me?" Dan asked cheerfully, "just as friends, of course," he added as though he could read her mind..

"Dan, that's really sweet, but I really don't feel like going out tonight. The restaurants are going to be too crowded and I'm just not in the mood to be around people right now."

"That's okay." Dan responded. "I get it. Maybe we can do it next week when things have calmed down."

Olivia could hear the sadness and hurt in Dan's voice. But...Olivia was telling the truth when she said she did not want to face crowds of people. She needed to be in her own home right now. Yet, Dan was her best friend and he did say just as friends. Would it be so hard to have dinner with a dear friend? "Listen. What if you come over here instead and I'll make a fast dinner?"

Dan readily accepted, knowing he was in for a treat with Olivia cooking. Even meatloaf tasted better when she made it.

Olivia was busy searing salmon when Dan walked in the door. He gave her a kiss on the cheek and was just hanging up his coat when the phone rang. Olivia called out, "Dan, can you get that please? I'm at a point I can't stop."

"No problem."

A minute later Dan came back into the kitchen, an odd look on his face. Olivia looked up. "Who was it?"

"Alex. But he sounded strange; almost startled that I answered the phone. Said he was just calling to make sure you were okay. I said you seemed to be then he said good bye and hung up. He didn't even ask to speak with you."

Olivia's heart leapt like a schoolgirl's at the mention of Alex. She looked at Dan, foolishly feeling guilty. She kicked herself and told herself she had nothing to feel guilty about. Dan was not her boyfriend. Anyway, she didn't know if that kiss meant anything more than just that, a stolen kiss. And, she reminded herself, Alex was still the enemy.

Dan looked at her silently. Something about her seemed different. Despite all the problems of the past week, she almost glowed.

"Why is Alex, of all people, worrying about you?" he asked finally.

Not looking Dan in the eye, she turned back to sauté potatoes and said as coolly as she could, "He bumped into me while I was at the store today, then came over here for coffee. We talked about things for a while. I thought maybe I could convince him to put his store somewhere else."

Dan looked at Olivia with her back to him as she spoke about Alex. Something definitely had changed. Suspiciously, he wondered what was going on between the two of them. He knew he had no claim on Olivia, but jealousy still snaked its way into his heart.

"You seem to be getting along with him."

"On some level, yes. But, I'm still concerned that his business will impact mine," she replied honestly. "He said he wanted to talk to me when he got back from Chicago. I don't know what he wants to talk to me about. I certainly do not want to be part of his empire." As she said this aloud, a thought crossed her mind. What if Alex had been trying to butter her up in order to make it easier to get her out of his way? That was the only rational explanation for his actions. She was sure of it.

"So it's all business?"

Olivia shot him a look. Uncomfortably she said, "Yes. Definitely."

"Good, because I need to talk to you about the other night."

"Dan...you promised," she said, putting the potatoes in the warming oven.

"No, Olivia. We have to talk. You have been my best friend for years, but I've loved you from the very beginning. Even when you were with Michael. But, I knew then that you two belonged together. Olivia, Michael's gone. At some point you are going to have to accept that he's not coming back." Dan wished that hadn't come out as brutally as it sounded.

Olivia stood up, turned around and really looked at Dan. His azure eyes behind his glasses were serious with a hint of anger in them. She went up to him and drew his mouth to hers, giving him a long kiss. She felt him returning the kiss with warmth, but there was no enchantment, no fire. Quietly, Olivia stepped back and again looked into Dan's eyes. There she read the depth of his sadness. Clearly, he had felt the emptiness of their kiss. Whatever magic it was that sparked passion between two people was not there and he could not conjure it up by himself. He had told her it was time to realize Michael was not coming back, when really he should have been telling himself it was time to realize Olivia would never be his. He brushed a curl back tenderly from her forehead and said, "You're right. It was wrong of me to say that. Can we still be friends, or have I totally ruined our relationship?"

"I would love it if we could stay friends. You are one of the dearest people in my life. Now I'm starving. Can we eat?"

Chapter 11

Alex sat alone in his elegant townhouse in Chicago, nursing a Scotch. He missed the company and comfort of Buster, who had remained behind in a fancy kennel in Connecticut. It would not have been fair to drag him on two flights just for a few days. His mind traveled to Connecticut. Why should Dan not have been at Olivia's when he'd called? Hearing his voice had startled and shaken him. It made total sense that he would be there; after all, Olivia was his girlfriend. Was he to imitate what his own best friend had done to him and steal Dan's girlfriend away from him? Granted, they weren't married, but it was close enough.

He could still feel the kiss on his lips, and when he closed his eyes, he could smell the faint perfume of Olivia's lavender soap on her skin. She had felt the electricity too, he was sure of it. Nevertheless, that only made him more determined to keep his distance and remain businesslike. Dan was a good guy and would make a fine husband for Olivia. He didn't want to interfere in either of their lives, no matter how much it hurt. He would not allow himself to get involved with Olivia. Alex shook his head. The fact that those words even crossed his mind startled him.

After a sleepless night, Alex drove over to European Gourmet's corporate office. His assistant, Tony, was ready for him when he arrived. A pile of documents, neatly stacked on his mahogany desk, awaited him. Alex started flipping through the papers, then impatiently pushed them aside, and got up to go to the window. Looking out over the snow covered rooftops of the city, he lost himself in the memory of Olivia lying in the snow the day Buster knocked her down. She had been enchanting. Disgusted, he wondered why he insisted on torturing himself.

    Abruptly turning around, he caught Tony watching him curiously. Briskly he said, "Arrange a meeting for this afternoon with the acquisitions team."

    "Absolutely. Will do. Anything else on your mind, Alex? Anything I can help with?"

    "Thanks Tony, but I'm fine. Just the usual things to think about," he lied.

    "Well, let me know if you need anything," said Tony as he left to organize the meeting. Alex sat back down at his desk, clicked on his computer, and started to download the store's holiday statistics. Sales looked very soft compared to the previous year, and certainly not up to budget projections. The economy was finally taking a toll on the business, despite the moves they had made to hedge against it. They'd have to be smarter and conserve cash to weather this storm. He'd have to balance the risk of expansion with the need to preserve assets. Real estate was very attractive right now. It was definitely the right time from that point of view. He decided to call his father in New Mexico, where he had retired, to talk things over. His father was still sharp as a tack and the best business advisor he could possibly ask for.

He dialed the number and was pleased to hear a hearty hello come through the receiver.

"Hi Dad, I thought I'd give a call to see how you and Mom were doing now that the holidays are over. I also need to discuss a couple of business items with you, if you have a minute."

"Well hello, Alex. It's nice to hear from you. Your mother and I are great. You can't complain about eighty dry degrees and plenty of sunshine. We missed you this past week. The holidays aren't the same without you, but we know how busy you are. What's going on in the business world that you need to talk about?"

"I'd like to send you the sales reports and balance sheet, if you don't mind. You know real estate is very cheap right now and we could scoop up some amazing properties for almost nothing, but sales are soft. I'm meeting with the team this afternoon, but I sure would like your input if you had a moment. I'm also rethinking the expansion into Connecticut."

"I thought the team did a pretty thorough job analyzing the idea of expansion there and was all for it. What did they miss?"

"Well," he hesitated, "the competition is a little more complicated than we had anticipated."

"Competition never bothered you before. What's different here?"

"I'm not sure. Listen. Take a look at the numbers. I've got a meeting this afternoon at three with everyone. Any chance we could talk before then?"

"Well, I'm flattered you still value an old man's opinion. I've got nothing going on today but a golf game and this is much more interesting. I'll call you in your office at two."

"Perfect. Thanks, Dad." Alex hung up and looked out the window. Where were the brutal clarity and decision making abilities that he was so well known for?

For the next few hours, Alex buried himself in work, with only an occasional thought of Olivia floating unbidden through his mind. The way her hair looked tied up in its floppy bow, how she smelled of vanilla and lavender, and tasted of....

He shook himself mentally. He was *not* going to get involved romantically with anyone right now. Certainly not with a person whom he was most likely going to have to have tough negotiations with; and certainly not with someone who was in a relationship with another man.

At 2 pm his father called and all thoughts of Olivia were put temporarily on hold.

Chapter 12

Olivia and Harry worked companionably together in the empty store, standing on stepladders counting banks of bottles and jars, completing the end of year inventory. Bundled up against the cold, Olivia still shivered while entering product codes and quantities into the scanning gun she held. Jazz quietly played in the background as she and Harry methodically moved from item to item. She was pleased at how little inventory remained on the shelves. The holidays had truly gone well.

"Hey, Harry, how's it going with John?"

"I almost don't want to talk about it for fear of jinxing things – but it's going great. It's too soon to tell if it'll last, but right now I'm loving it."

Olivia looked at Harry contentedly working beside her. Sharp and witty when it came to work, she suspected he was naïve when it came to his personal life. How could she shield him from getting hurt again? The last guy sounded terrifying. "Well it's about time you found a nice guy. I still haven't met him, you know. Hint, hint," she smiled.

Harry rolled his eyes. "Lordy Lou! You'd think you were my mother!"

"No. Just watching out for a friend. Has Tommy surfaced since the other night?"

"No, thank God. If it weren't for John, I'd be a nervous wreck."

"What do you mean?"

"Well, remember what he said last Christmas Eve about getting me? I didn't tell you, but the first time he threatened to hurt me was on the night we broke up. Luckily, all my friends were there and they threatened to hurt him even more if he hurt me. Geez! Who would have thought that a nice-looking guy like him would turn into such a creep?"

"Wow! You never told me this. And you think I'm overprotective? I should have been asking more questions!"

"Yeah, well, I think I learned my lesson. Anyway, what's new with you? Did they figure out who broke the window?"

"They called on Saturday and said they had prints, but no match. They're still working on it. I just hope nothing more happens. They did say they were patrolling the store to keep an eye on it."

Just then, a scraping sound could be heard near the kitchen window by the back door. She assumed it was Gus Mancarella coming to fix the front window, so she climbed down from the stepladder and headed towards the door to let him in. She paused by the kitchen window to signal that she was on her way to open the door and saw not Gus, but the back of a smaller man wearing a red baseball cap hurrying up the hill of the parking lot. Startled, she stood still for a moment, the hair rising on the back of her neck in some primal response to a fear she could not identify. She hurried to the back door, opened it quickly and looked out. The man had disappeared. Cautiously she stepped into the parking lot, but it was no one was in sight. Puzzled, she walked back into the store, carefully locking the door behind her.

"Harry, some guy was just here looking in the window. I didn't get a good look at him, because he ran up the hill just as I went to open the door. Don't ask me why, but he gave me the creeps!"

Harry came down from his ladder to the back window to see if he could see anyone. The parking lot was deserted. "Looks like whoever it was, was in a hurry to get away. Do you have any idea who it might have been?"

"No. He seemed slightly familiar somehow, but I didn't see his face. I can't tell if I'm just being paranoid, or what."

"Right now being paranoid is not a bad reaction," said Harry. "Look what's happened so far!"

They got back to work on the inventory, each lost in their own thoughts.

A few moments later she heard another tap at the back window, and this time the friendly face of Gus Mancarella peered in. She hurried to open the back door. Grateful to see a friendly face, she surprised him by giving him an enthusiastic hug.

"Well, I'd be a happy man if all my customers greeted me that way!" he exclaimed.

Olivia laughed. "I'm just happy to see you. Come on in. Maybe your guys should park the truck around the front, so you'll be closer to the window."

"Good idea. I'll go tell them. Be back in a sec."

Olivia went to open the front door for the men when, as she opened it, she noticed an old Toyota being driven by a man wearing a red baseball cap pulling away from the curb. "Harry! Come here! I think the man I saw is in a car in front of the store!" Harry hustled down from the ladder and ran to the front of the store. The car by now had pulled up to the red light a little ways down the street. Just as Harry looked out, the light turned green and the car turned around the corner out of sight. Harry blanched visibly. Olivia looked at him. "What? Do you know him?"

"Maybe," he answered feebly. "That car looked suspiciously like that of my dear insane ex, Tommy. Oh, God…and we were just talking about him."

He sat down heavily on the nearest coffee bar stool.

"Wow, Harry. He must really have had a thing for you. Understandably, of course," she said with a weak smile.

"Just when I thought my life was perfect," moaned Harry.

"Everything alright?" asked Gus, as he walked in the door.

Hesitantly Olivia answered, "Yes…, I think so. We just thought we saw an old acquaintance. It's nothing important."

"Well, we'll have this window looking better than new in no time. Then your store won't be so cold!"

Olivia smiled at him weakly. "Thanks, Gus. You're a godsend."

"All in a day's work," replied Gus, walking over to put his tools down by the blinded window.

Olivia turned back to Harry, who was still sitting on the stool, a worried expression in his eyes. "Harry, let's be realistic. What could Tommy do to you? Whatever Tommy was doing hanging around here doesn't matter. Let him stalk you, if that's what he needs. You are in an exciting new relationship, it's a new year, and no one is going to hurt you. And, you're always welcome to stay at my place, if you are really worried,"

Harry got up and gave Olivia a hug. "Thanks. You're too sweet. I'm lucky to have you as a friend."

Olivia stepped back and looked at him thoughtfully. "Why don't you call the police and at least let them know about Tommy's threat and that you saw him today. Yes, I know, they won't be able to do anything, but at least they'll be aware of him. Who knows, he might be such a creep that he's done something to someone else."

Harry pondered the idea for a moment, then said decidedly, "You're right. It won't hurt to let them know. I'll call right now, then I'll come back to finish this," he said waving his arms expansively around the room.

Three hours later, she and Harry had managed to work their way around most of the store, while Gus had finished putting in the window. Light poured through the new pane, and the store had warmed up by several degrees.

Gus sheepishly handed her the bill saying, "I feel terrible having to charge you, but I got to. Have you tried getting insurance to pay this? They might, you know. Sometimes these things are covered under your policy."

Olivia took the bill and gave him a quick smile. "You are very sweet. Don't worry about the bill, insurance will most likely cover most of it. Anyway, you have to make a living, too. And it was so nice of you to fix it so promptly."

Gus and his men left, leaving Olivia and Harry to finish counting the last corner of the store. She felt relieved that her store was whole again, but couldn't shake the feeling that something was not quite right. Some vague idea was hidden in the back of her mind, but wouldn't come forward.

Putting the last bottle back on the shelf, Olivia looked at Harry and said, "That's it for this year! Harry, I think we need to rethink our strategies for the coming year. Could you call the staff to let them know there will be a short meeting tomorrow after closing? I'd like to brainstorm a few things."

"Sure thing. I'll get on it right away," he responded. "It would be fun to do something different. Not that it hasn't been fun already, of course," he added with the twinkle returning to his eyes.

At home that night, the phone rang just as Olivia tucked herself under the bedcovers. Glancing at the clock on the bedside table, she wondered who could be calling so late. Her heart jumped for a second, as a brief thought flitted through her mind, then she saw Dan's number on the phone.

Tiredly she said, "Hi, Dan. What's up?"

Dan heard the hint of disappointment in her voice. He swallowed a sigh and said, "Not much. I was just thinking about you and was wondering how you were doing with the store."

"The store is back to normal and the window is fixed, so I'm ok." She hesitated, then said, "Do you remember Harry's old boyfriend?"

"Sure, I remember him. He wasn't a very savory character, as far as I knew. Why? Is Harry getting back together with him?"

Feeling foolish, Olivia said, "No, far from it! But...today, I thought I saw him staring into the back window. When I heard a noise back there, I went to see what was going on. I think he saw me and turned around and ran up the hill. I'm not positive it was him, though, but whoever it was, was wearing a red baseball cap. Next thing I knew, a person with a red baseball cap was pulling out of a parking space in the front of the store, driving away as fast as he could. He had to stop at the light and that's when Harry saw the car and thought it was Tommy's old car. He didn't see the driver, though, so he's not positive it was him. It's funny. We had just been talking about him and how he was such a creep, threatening to hurt Harry when they broke up."

"Did you call the police and tell them about this?"

"Yes, well, I didn't. Harry did." Olivia glanced out the window, her eyes pulled by an unexpected light in the distance. "Dan, I think I just saw a light in the window of the Mere's mansion!"

"What? How is that possible? The sale hasn't gone through yet. Is there any way Alex could be over there at this time of night?"

"I don't think so. He's supposed to be in Chicago." She watched as the light moved shakily from one window to the next. "Dan, I think whoever it is, is using a flashlight. The light is not steady and it's moving around. As far as I know, the electricity isn't on over there. Maybe someone broke in and is just camping out. I think I'm going to call the police. It feels like I should have them on speed-dial these days!"

Olivia watched the moving light and could feel the worried pause that floated through the phone. Finally, Dan said, "Olivia, I really wish you would sleep over here tonight. I would feel so much better, knowing you were safe. Even if that is just a squatter over there, you still could be in danger."

"I'll be fine. The police will come by and they'll check everything out. I really don't want to sleep somewhere else tonight. I have to get up early in the morning and all my stuff is here."

"Well, if you won't come over here, do you mind if I come over there? I really don't like the idea of you being alone. I won't bother you, I promise. It would just make me feel better."

Olivia thought about having Dan in the house overnight. He really was being sweet, and she had to admit, it would be nice to have someone else there tonight. She smiled and said, "You've always been my knight in shining armor. If you insist, you can come over and sleep here. The guest room bed is already made up. I'll call the police to have them check things out. See you soon…and thank you."

"I'll be over in about half an hour. See you then."

Olivia hung up and looked at the phone. She should be madly in love with this wonderful man. Maybe she could make an effort. She dearly loved Dan, but…with a sigh, she swung her legs out of the bed and put her bathrobe on before heading to the kitchen to call the police. Again.

The sergeant took her call seriously and said a cruiser would be over in five minutes to check out the situation. Olivia put the phone down slowly. Unbidden, thoughts of Alex entered her mind again. She picked up the receiver and found the number that was logged on caller ID the night Dan had answered the phone. She wrote it down on the notepad she kept for those inspired ideas that woke her in the middle of the night. Putting down the receiver again, she looked at the number thoughtfully. Was Alex really in Chicago? Was it possible he had said that to her to put her off her guard?

Olivia put a kettle of water on to make herself a cup of chamomile tea while waiting for Dan to arrive. As the water heated, she went back to her notepad. She stared at the telephone number again, and then suddenly decided. She just had to know. Trembling, she called the number. A recording of Alex's clipped voice answered. Olivia was about to hang up when the recording abruptly cut off and was replaced by Alex's very real voice. In a panic, she pressed the "End" button, just as the doorbell rang. She ran to the door to find Dan there toting his backpack.

"You look like a school boy on his way to a sleepover," she smiled shakily.

"I feel like a friend protecting a friend in danger," he replied grumpily.

"You're right. I am not taking this lightly. You just looked so sweet standing there in the doorway."

Throwing his bag onto the sofa he asked, "Have the police come by yet?"

Olivia shook her head. "Not yet. Dan, I have to confess something. I got Alex's number from caller ID and just called him in Chicago to make sure he was there. His answering machine came on. I was just hanging up when I heard his voice. So whoever is in the house is not Alex."

"Did you ask him if he had someone staying at the house?"

"No...o...o... I ...I just hung up when I heard his voice."

Dan looked at her quizzically. "Olivia, if you weren't my best friend I'd say you'd lost your marbles. Well, anyway, at least we know he's not here. That's something. Show me where you saw the lights."

They were just moving over to Olivia's living room window when the phone rang. They looked at each other. Dan said, "Are you expecting any calls?"

Olivia shook her head.

"I'll get it then" He went over, looked at the unidentified number on caller id, and picked up the phone. "Hello?"

There was a pause, then Alex said, "Dan? Is that you? Did you just call me?"

"Hi, Alex."

Olivia spun around when she heard Alex's name and a blush began to creep up her neck.

Dan looked over at her and continued. "No, I didn't call; it was Olivia. But, I think she thought you were asleep when she got your answering machine, so hung up."

"Is anything wrong?"

"Well, I wouldn't say wrong exactly; puzzling might be a better word. Look, why don't I have you speak with her directly and she can explain. Here she is." Dan said as he handed the phone over to Olivia.

Olivia shook her head silently at Dan, then took the phone from him and went over to sit on the couch. Taking a deep breath she said, "Hi Alex. I'm sorry to have bothered you when you were sleeping."

"It's no bother at all; I wasn't sleeping," he said softly. "Now, tell me what's going on."

"When I was on the phone earlier this evening, I noticed a light moving around in the Meres mansion. It seemed like an odd time for someone to be exploring the place and you said you were going to Chicago for a few days. I didn't know what to think, after all the events at my store."

Alex listened in disbelief. "Who the hell could be in the mansion?"

Olivia sighed. "I don't know. I called the police, so they should be over at the mansion to check things out pretty soon, if they haven't come already."

Alex paused a moment, then said, "I'm going to catch a flight back tomorrow and find out what's going on. I'll get in touch with you at some point tomorrow afternoon. When you see the police, can you please give them my number? I'd like to speak with them. And Olivia…one day you will learn you can trust me. Say good night to Dan for me." Abruptly, he hung up.

Damn the man! Could he read her mind? Olivia looked over at Dan who was watching her curiously and said, "So Alex is in Chicago. That climinates one suspect. He's going to fly back tomorrow. He wants me to give the police his phone number."

"I saw the police go into the mansion while you were on the phone. You have to get up earlier than I do. Why don't you go to bed, and I'll wait up for them? I'll leave you a note if they say anything of importance."

Olivia looked at Dan. There were circles under his eyes. He had worked hard all day and did not need this. "No, Dan. You're beat and need sleep, too."

"I won't be able to sleep. No use having two tired people tomorrow. I'm serious. Go to bed. I'll stay up. If we need you, we'll come and get you." He took her by the shoulders, gently spun her around, and gave her a tender shove in the direction of the stairs.

Olivia shook her head and stopped protesting. As she started up the stairs she looked back down into his caring eyes and said quietly, "Thank you, my fearless protector. As always, you are a dear. I probably should go to bed, though how I'm going to sleep is beyond me. You know where the guest room is. Help yourself to anything in the refrigerator. I'll probably be gone by the time you wake up since I'm leaving at 5am, so I'll call you sometime tomorrow to see what's up."

Dan looked at her. After a moment he said, "Goodnight."

Olivia reached over the banister and gave him a quick kiss on the nose, ignoring the look in his eyes, and left him with his thoughts to wait for the police to come by and report.

Chapter 13

The afternoon meeting with the team, coupled with his father's advice, confirmed that the next logical step for the company was to build this central location in Connecticut. Not only was it the right location, but the timing of the real estate deal was perfect. Even if business remained soft, the value of the real estate would increase dramatically over time. He could not let his attraction to a young female storeowner distract him. But this business with the mansion was disconcerting. Business or not, he did not like the idea of Olivia being in any kind of danger. It was curious that Olivia had two attacks on her business and now someone had broken in just by her house. Did someone have it out for her? Alex finished his business in Chicago and flew into New York the next afternoon. He took a limousine up his uncle's house where the housekeeper greeted him with a smile.

"Welcome back, Alex. We were not expecting you until Thursday."

Alex nodded and said, "I had a quick change of plans. I'm just going to go up and change, then I'll be out the rest of the day. Could you please let my uncle know I'm back when he comes in?

"Certainly. Let me know if you need anything."

Alex opened the door to his suite to find the taupe room neat and smelling sweetly of cedar. He deposited his briefcase on the desk, loosened his tie with a sigh of relief, and glanced at his cell phone as he quickly changed into his jeans. No new messages. The police had been over at the Meres property the night before. He had hoped for some information by now about the intruder, but none had been forthcoming. The thought of stopping by Olivia's store crossed his mind. He could get a cup of coffee and see if she had any new information. Alex laughed at himself. Really? He could just as easily call the police and get more information that way. Who was he fooling? All he wanted to do was to talk to Olivia again.

   He needed to stay away from her. She was involved with Dan, so he was not going to attempt to steal her away, and he had business plans that still needed to be fine-tuned. He finished tying on his boots, grabbed his keys, and decided to pick up Buster at the kennel before setting off for the mansion. On the way, he would give a call to the police to find out what was going on.

Chapter 14

Olivia woke up at five the next morning to find a note on the counter from Dan saying the police had found tire tracks next to the mansion and that the back kitchen door had been forced open. The police would patrol the mansion and her house throughout the day. Olivia felt a knot of fear tighten in her stomach. It probably was just a squatter, but it felt like a destructive force was moving closer to her,…or was she simply becoming paranoid? At the moment, she could do nothing about it. She wrote a thank you note to Dan, promising to call him at work later in the day, and left it next to a coffeecake by the coffee machine. Right now, she had a business to run and a future to think of.

Four hours later, Olivia found herself sitting at the small table in the front of the store listening to the enthusiastic plans of one of her most important customers. Shelves of photograph albums of catered events, books of past menus, and cookbooks lined the wall behind the imposing woman. Claire Austin was a force to be reckoned with. As the town's matriarch, she set the trends and blessed the businesses with her approval, leading a flock of followers to their doors – leaving the unsupported to struggle with fewer customers. Today, she had woken up and decided that the new year meant healthy menus and local food. Claire declared that the town needed classes on how to prepare such fare and menus to cater their special events that would allow them to indulge without being unhealthy. She was tired of being entertained with food that added inches to her waistline and did nothing for the local economy. Claire decided that it was Olivia who would develop these ideas, and she would make sure to send all her friends her way.

Olivia managed to tamp down the irritation she felt and looked thoughtfully at the exquisitely manicured woman before her. Admittedly, she was pompous and bossy, but you had to give it to her; she had her pulse on the trends. Sweet Sage already provided menus made from healthy, local ingredients, but Olivia knew she did not publicize that fact loudly enough. This would be a way to herald all the good things already produced in the kitchen. The thought of hiring a web developer to help her with an on-line cooking school had already crossed her mind and Claire was simply nudging…no, pushing…her in the right direction. Perhaps she would even write a cookbook to go along with the cooking classes. She felt the excitement building as her mind raced from one possibility to another. "Claire, I think these are wonderful ideas. They are right in line with Sweet Sage's philosophy and goals," she responded diplomatically.

"Well, then. We're in agreement. Now, what I really came to speak with you about is that my daughter is getting married in June. The wedding will be at my house, of course. This would be the perfect occasion to show what you can do. Put together some menus for me to look at. Ella comes home from Paris in the spring. She will want to come by for a wedding cake tasting. Of course, she has her ideas of what the cake should look like. I'll forward photos she sent. Her fiancé is French, so they will be splitting their time between Paris and Connecticut. Being French, they know good food. I don't want to disappoint them. The food must be exquisite. The service must be impeccable. I have hired the top wedding planner from New York to insure everything is perfect." Claire took a breath, allowing a bemused Olivia to finally get a word in.

"Congratulations! That's very exciting. I'd be happy to put together some menus. What day in June were you planning to have the wedding?"

"Of course, how silly of me. June 24th. It will be an evening wedding. We will most likely have around 300 guests with many dignitaries present. Ella's fiancé's family is heavily involved in the government in France." Claire eyed Olivia sharply. "You have done a superb job on all my events to date, but this is different. It must be perfect. I need your assurance that nothing will go wrong. And be honest. I expect you to tell me if you are not capable of something of this magnitude."

Olivia sensed the shift in Claire. This supremely confident woman was feeling the pressure to perform well for her daughter in front of the new in-laws...and Olivia felt the tension. This was not going to be an easy event. Could she and her staff handle it? It had the potential to break her business, if there were any disasters. She thought back over the elegant weddings she had put on in the last few years. They had run seamlessly. What was so different this time? Yes, they could do it, she was sure of it.

Olivia looked the woman straight in her eyes. "We can do it, Claire. You know we can, or you wouldn't be here asking me to do it. Your daughter's wedding will be magnificent. Have your planner give me a call and I'll put together some ideas. Give me a call when Ella is ready for the cake tasting."

Claire looked at the young woman sitting across from her. Her eyes were clear and honest. With a satisfied nod she said, "Good. I'll tell my planner to call you. His name is Edward Maddox. You have probably heard of him. We need to schedule a tasting of the menu. That can be done before Ella arrives. She is more concerned about the cake. I, on the other hand, am more interested in the menu. Please schedule it with Edward."

Olivia had heard rumors about Maddox, and they were not terribly flattering. Apparently, he could be a gorgon toward staff and dictatorial when dealing with the caterer. This could be a challenge.

Claire continued, "And don't forget about local and healthy cuisine. Let me know when you have any classes that I can send my cook to." She rose imperiously and buttoned up her finely tailored golden wool coat.

Olivia rose and joined her as she headed towards the front door. "I'll give you a call when the cooking classes are scheduled." She smiled at Claire.

"Your daughter's wedding will be a pleasure to execute. There is nothing we would like better than to put it on and knock some socks off!"

Claire returned a small smile and replied, "Thank you. Edward will be in touch."

Olivia watched the woman walk out the front door and nearly skipped back to the kitchen. Harry quickly came in behind her.

"What was all that about?" he asked.

"Harry, we're off to a brilliant start to the year. Claire Austin wants us to cater her daughter's wedding in June, and she wants us to run cooking classes for the town! With her stamp of approval, everyone will follow her lead."

"Well, it's not like everyone is not coming already!" Harry huffed.

Olivia soothed him, "I know we're doing well, but if we want to keep growing, we have to keep pushing ourselves into new areas and always get better at what we do. This will just help us do that. I've got so many ideas that my mind is spinning."

Gilberta had come over to listen. "This sounds exciting, but how are we going to do it all? We don't have that big a staff, and you are only one person."

Olivia grinned. "You're right. This will take careful planning. It might mean taking on new people, but I do need to be cautious. We've come so far. I don't want to jeopardize it by taking on too many new expenses, but sometimes you need to take a risk," she said her mind wandering again to all the possibilities.

Harry grinned at Gilberta. "Looks like our fearless leader is already working on it. Come on. Let's get back to work and let her think."

Olivia smiled gratefully at them and went down to her office. Broken windows, smashed vents, and lights in old mansions did not even enter her mind as she started to work on her ideas.

Chapter 15

Alex drove slowly down the road to the Meres mansion. His glance traveled, as though pulled by magnets, to the small stone cottage sitting peacefully not a half mile away from the big house. Again, unbidden, his thoughts went back to Olivia and the same electrical charge betrayed him, coursing through him like molten lava. Just then, the front door of the cottage opened and Alex saw Dan walk out towards the car that was nearly hidden on the side of the little house, closing the door carefully behind him. Alex swore under his breath and pressed the gas pedal to the floor.

The police were waiting for him when he drove up to the house. They walked inside. The house was still and a chill dustiness filled the air. When he had first seen it, the sunshine had filled the high ceilinged rooms and there had been an aura of elegant times past, or so he had imagined. He also had imagined settling down here, perhaps…, in time, with a family around him. Today, he laughed at himself derisively, mocking himself for having given in to such romantic notions.

"Looks like whoever was here was planning on camping out for a period of time. There's a bag of food and some belongings by the fireplace in the big front room. Other than the back door, nothing looks to be more damaged than it already was," the trim policewoman interrupted his thoughts.

"Do you have any idea who this person might be?" asked Alex.

"Well, we have prints from the back door, so we'll run them through the database. Until we do that, we really can't tell. There are tire tracks in the snow, too, so we'll take a look at those. If I were you, I would get new locks on the doors. We'll keep patrolling, but honestly, this is a little out of our way and we won't be able to cover this area every hour of the day."

"I appreciate everything you've done so far," said Alex. "I've put a bid on the property, but it's not mine yet. I'll have the agent get those locks changed today. There is one more thing; I am a little concerned about the safety of the owner of that stone house down the road."

"That's Olivia Caron's house, right? The owner of Sweet Sage?"

"That's right. You do realize her store has been vandalized twice already in the last two weeks? Could this be related, do you think?"

The policewoman looked thoughtful. "It's possible, though truly, this looks like someone just crashing in an empty house. We'll know more after we run the fingerprints. But, you're right...I'll see what I can do about beefing up the patrol in the area. Let's keep in touch." With a nod, she walked back with her partner to the car.

Alex watched as the police cruiser drove out the driveway. He was angry...angry at himself... angry at Dan...angry at the intruder. Abruptly, he turned around, got into his car and drove back to town, heading for the real estate office that had shown him the property. Two hours later, he was sitting in his uncle's study, preparing his plan of attack for installing the eastern seaboard flagship store. He had gotten sidetracked, but he was back on course.

Chapter 16

Olivia sat at the coffee bar, her head nearly touching the dark head of the young woman sitting next to her as they pored over a laptop, oblivious to everything around them. It had not taken long for Olivia to find a talented web designer. Gilberta's younger sister Marta, nearly finished with her computer programming degree, needed a shining example of a sophisticated webpage on her resume if she hoped to get hired by the big guns. This was the perfect vehicle. The two women had instantly bonded and were now spending hours in the small basement office working on concepts and designs for the website and cooking videos. Luckily, Marta was on winter break and business had slowed in the store to a manageable pace after the holidays. Gilberta and Harry checked in on the two occasionally, as they kept the store humming along smoothly. A week later, with the sun glittering in the winter cold, the office had become claustrophobic. Olivia had moved them upstairs, despite the possibility of distractions and interruptions.

Now, Olivia sat up with a satisfied smile. "That just about does it for a start! Next, we need to start filming the videos." Her excitement fairly bubbled out of her.

"I have a friend who makes great videos. He'd like to earn a little cash. I bet he'd be happy to film a couple of videos before school gets back in," said Marta.

"That would be perfect! Why don't you call him while I talk with Harry and Gilberta to see if they would be interested in helping." Pausing, she hopped off her stool and gave Marta a big hug. "Oh, Marta! Thank you so much for your wonderful work. This is going to be so much fun!"

Marta grinned as Olivia went back to the kitchen to talk with Harry and Gilberta.

Gilberta, with the help of an earnest young cook, was pulling sheets of golden pasta out from the pasta roller. A bowl of lump crab filling sat nearby, waiting to be stuffed into the newly rolled dough. Olivia waved Harry over as he came through the door. "Hey, can I bother the two of you for a minute?"

"Sure. Robby, please cover this up and we'll finish when I get back and could you please finish up the soup?" asked Gilberta of the young cook by the stove while wiping her hands on the towel hanging at her waist.

" No problem," the young man nodded.

Gilberta and Harry followed Olivia downstairs to the office. Olivia shut the door behind them. She was fairly bouncing on her toes. "We're done with the website template. Of course, we're going to need to load inventory into the web store, add recipes to the cooking class files, and film cooking class videos before we launch it. It would be great if we could get a couple of videos filmed before Marta has to go back to school. Would you two be interested in helping out with filming a couple of classes? You'd end up on the video, of course, so you'd be seen on the web. Who knows, you might get famous!"

Harry and Gilberta laughed.

"Wow. You and Marta really accomplished a lot this week. Being part of a cooking video would be a blast," said Harry. "I love watching all those dishy guys whipping up stuff. I know just what to wear."

Gilberta gave him a withering look. Worriedly, she turned to Olivia. "We need to clean the kitchen better than ever and prep everything. What recipes were you going to start with? I'm happy to help and it would be fun to be part of this, but I'm worried about having the time to do everything. I know we're slow, but we do have a couple of events coming up."

Olivia looked at her thoughtfully. Leave it to Gilberta to worry, but, she had to admit Gilberta had a point; it was one thing for her to take over for Olivia for a few days, it was another thing to add to the workload on top of it. "I think we're going to have to beef up hours for a few staff while we are working on this. Hopefully, when the classes and the on-line store take off we'll have the money to hire more staff." Thankfully, the holidays had been good to the store. Despite the damaged hood and window, the small store had made a tidy profit. This would go far towards funding the new projects, but she still had to be careful. "Go ahead and arrange the schedules as you see fit. Let's try to film this coming Monday and

Wednesday after work. I'll get the recipes together and I'll prep on Sunday. Sound good?"

"You go girl!" crowed Harry. "Hollywood, here we come!"

Gilberta was more sedate, but her excitement shone in her dark eyes. "I'll start working on schedules right away. This could be a lot of fun. And, who knows...you might become the next Julia Childs!"

Olivia opened the office door. "Nothing can stop us now. Not this team." Behind her, the phone rang. She turned to the others and said, "I'll just take this and be up in a minute." Olivia picked up the phone. It was Dan.

"Hey. Just thought I'd check in and see how you were doing."

"Hi, Dan. Things are great, and I'm having so much fun. The website is almost ready to launch and we start filming cooking videos next week!" she bubbled.

"Wow! You move fast. Hey, the real reason I called was to give you some news about the mansion."

Olivia shook her head. The mansion? The mansion seemed like another reality...so far away. She had nearly forgotten about all the problems that had surfaced over the holidays. Creating and turning ideas into reality with a group of fantastic people absorbed all her thoughts and energy. Hearing the mansion mentioned jolted back worries that had managed to recede far into the background. Where was Alex these days, anyways? Why hadn't she heard from him?

"Olivia?" You there?" asked Dan.

"Hmm...Yes. Just thinking. Did they find the person who broke in?"

"I haven't heard about that, but that's not what I wanted to tell you. The Meres mansion is back on the market. Alex must have gotten spooked by that break-in and decided not to buy it."

Olivia stood in stunned silence. Her mansion was on the market again? Maybe that's why she had not heard from Alex. He never contacted her to let her know what had happened at the house. Thinking of him now made her realize that she had not thought of him in almost a week. Annoyingly, the memory of the kiss sent shivers through her, while the nagging threat of competition from European Gourmet, temporarily put aside, also came back. Nevertheless, hadn't Alex promised he would not hurt her? Or, had he? Damn it! The store was going to soar in no time. She knew that the world of the internet leveled the playing field and she could feel that she had something special with her website. She just knew it would work. Let European Gourmet come to town. Claire Austin and the world would come to her.

Once again, her attraction to Alex intruded on her thoughts. "Damn it," she whispered unconsciously.

"Olivia, are you okay?" asked Dan.

"Yes. It's just that I've been very far away from all that this week. It's a shock to think about it again."

"I understand, but I thought this would be good news. You didn't seem happy with the idea of Alex buying the place."

"No. You're right, I wasn't. What is it on the market for this time?"

"Believe it or not, less than before. It seems like the owners really want to get rid of it now."

Olivia's thoughts careened wildly to all the possibilities. She had almost lost the mansion once. How could she prevent it from happening again?

"Dan, I have to go back to work. Can we talk later?"

"Of course. I have to go out of town tomorrow for a case. I should be back by the weekend. Could we get together Sunday?"

"I'm prepping for a shoot at the store on Sunday. Why don't you come by and be my food tester and we can talk?"

"Wild horses couldn't keep me away. See you then."

Olivia walked slowly back up to the kitchen lost in thought. Was there any way she could buy the mansion? And then what? Where would the money come from for renovating it? And what about all the new plans that were going to cost money to put into play? Anyway, what would she do with it? Rattle around in it by herself?

Chapter 17

Sunday came along with a brisk wind and the threat of more snow. Olivia hummed to herself in the quiet store kitchen as she made notes on her recipes and prepared the ingredients for the following evening's filming. The scent of roasted pumpkin and freshly baked almond tart shells wafted through the air. Olivia envisioned the first taste of the savory roasted pumpkin coconut soup on an unsuspecting tongue, followed by a crisp herb-stuffed chicken roasted with lemon parmesan cauliflower, and the grand finale, a lemon almond tart with freshly whipped cream and raspberries. Simple, quick, delicious, and healthy. She smiled. All that was needed was a table full of friends and family to share it with.

A sharp knock on the back window startled her out of her reverie. Dan stood there with a crimson and white scarf whipping about his head. Olivia ran to the back door to let him in. She was immediately engulfed in a hug that would have been warm if his coat hadn't been so cold.

"Br.r.r.r....Shut the door and come in! It's freezing out there!" exclaimed Olivia.

Dan shoved the door closed and followed Olivia into the kitchen. "Hmmm...Smells great in here. Anything to eat for a poor starving man?"

Olivia grinned. Dan was as thin as a rail, but always ready to eat. At least some things didn't change over the years. "I'm just about to finish a pumpkin coconut soup. Would you like to be my guinea pig and tell me honestly what you think of it?"

"Sure! Sounds delicious!"

Dan rested his jacket and scarf on a stool and took a seat on the stool next to the long steel table. He watched as Olivia whizzed the immersion blender through the ingredients simmering in the pot on the stove. A minute later, she put the blender down and set up two white porcelain bowls. A tray of freshly toasted shaved coconut sat nearby. Olivia ladled the golden soup into the bowls, then sprinkled a bit of the coconut shavings in the center of each fragrant pool, and handed Dan a spoon. "Be careful," she warned. "It's really hot."

Dan carefully accepted the bowl. The floral scent of ginger, coconut, and pumpkin assailed his nostrils. "This smells divine. It's so exotic; it's almost like a perfume."

Olivia smiled at him as she blew on her soupspoon to cool down the contents. "So tell me how your trip went."

"It was pretty routine. Nothing much to speak of; though it did go well. I'm more interested in what you've been up to. How's the website going?"

Olivia eyes glowed with excitement. "The site looks gorgeous. Clients can look up menus, order anything we sell in the store, and look for recipes. The recipes automatically give you the nutrition information and a shopping list. Marta is a genius!"

"How are you going to market the site?"

"Well, that *is* a good question. Marta says she know how to set us up so that when someone searches for a recipe or menu, Sweet Sage is one of the first search results that pops up. I hope she's right. I'm also going to call the newspaper and give them a heads up, sort of like a press release, to let them know about it. Hopefully, locals will be interested enough to look it up. I know Claire Austin is going to do her part to have her friends and her friends' cooks watch the videos once they are loaded on. If we get enough hits, we may attract advertisers."

Dan sipped his soup thoughtfully. "It sounds really good. It might start out slowly, but knowing you, it will catch on fast. By the way, in case you're wondering, this is delicious," he nodded at the vanishing soup.

Olivia tasted the soup herself. Unfortunately, she was more critical than Dan. Delicious as it was, it needed a little more kick; something to brighten it a little on the tongue. She would simmer a dried red chili and Thai basil in the coconut milk before adding the pumpkin in the next batch to see if that did the trick.

"Hey. What are you daydreaming of?" Dan asked. "Do you remember why I came over here?"

"You mean you came over here for another reason other than being fed?"

Dan looked into Olivia's cheerful face. It was so good to see her in high spirits again. He set the empty bowl down on the steel table. "Very funny. Maybe I'll just leave now, since you don't seem interested," he threatened, rising slightly from the stool.

"Okay, okay!" she laughed, grabbing him by the shoulders and forcing him to sit back down. "Yes, I do remember. It's hard to believe I've not thought about it since we talked on the phone. So, tell me everything you know."

"All I know is what Leo told me about his nephew. Apparently, Dumaurier had second thoughts and let the mansion go back on the market last Monday. The owners seem so fed up with the place that they've put it back on the market for almost nothing. At the price they're asking, it's almost worth buying just as an investment. I'm almost thinking of doing it myself."

Olivia's eyes widened. "Dan, you wouldn't?"

"I might. Why? Would that bother you?"

"No...o...o...," she said slowly, "though, to be honest, I was wondering if there was any way I could buy it. Don't ask me how I could afford it, or repair it."

Dan played with the spoon in the empty bowl. He had helped fund Olivia's store when she first started and that had been a worthwhile investment. "What were you thinking of doing with it?"

"I hadn't thought. I've been so busy with this project that the mansion, if you can believe it, slipped out of my mind. But, now that we're talking about it again, I have lots of ideas. For instance, I could start a cooking school with a small restaurant attached. We could put in a huge garden in the back and fix up the greenhouse to provide the kitchen with fresh herbs and some produce. It might be possible to have bed and breakfast rooms on the top floor." She stopped abruptly. *What an idiot. Where was she going to get the money for all this? Or the time?*

Dan looked at her quizzically.

Olivia heaved a sigh and asked, "If you bought it as an investment, what would you do with it?"

Dan looked at her thoughtfully. "Nothing as interesting as that. I just thought of having a contractor come in, fix it up, and sell it at a profit."

Silence fell in the small kitchen.

A glimmer of an idea began to form in Olivia's mind, just as a sharp rap at the back door jarred the calm. Startled, Olivia shot Dan a look.

"Stay here. I'll get it."

Olivia hurried to the back door and opened it to find her landlord, gnarled and disgruntled, standing there impatiently…with Alex at his side. Surprise flitted across her face as her eyes met Alex's steely ones. Their eyes locked.

Her landlord snapped, "Miss Caron, I didn't think there would be anyone in the building today, but seeing as you're here, maybe you can help me show Dumaurier around."

"Show him around?" Olivia repeated, uncomprehending, wrenching her eyes away.

"You hard of hearing? I said show him around. I'm selling the buildings on this block and Dumaurier is interested."

Olivia's jaw dropped. She felt a hand on her shoulder. Dan had walked over and now stood next to her as the cold wind whistled in through the door. "Why don't we all come in and shut the door?" he said, protectively keeping his arm around Olivia's shoulders, while pointedly looking at the older man.

Alex took in the protective stance. Anger radiated through him. Just as well this problem was going to be taken care of in the not too distant future. The last thing he needed was temptation in his way. This was business, nothing more, nothing personal. Once the deal was signed and construction had begun, the unpleasant aspects would disappear. They always did. Money would exchange hands and it was always interesting to notice how far that went to making things better.

Olivia gathered her wits. "I have a lease that prevents you from entering without my permission. Were you planning on sneaking in when I wasn't here? How many times have you done this? Technically, I could have you arrested for trespassing."

Hotchkiss glared at her. "This is still my property.

"Maybe. But as a tenant, I have my rights."

Dan looked at the landlord then at Alex, whose face betrayed no emotion. "Olivia's right. If I remember correctly, the lease stipulates twenty-four hours' notice to enter."

Bitterly, Olivia said, "It's okay Dan. Let them in. Better now than when we're not here." She whirled around and headed back to the kitchen. "Shut the door behind you."

Alex walked through the door behind the landlord and closed it firmly behind him. Looking around more carefully, he again noticed the well-swept floors, the neatly arranged wooden shelves, and the baskets of displayed goods. Attention was evident in every little detail despite the aging features, creating a quaint and charming space. The brick walls looked in good condition, but the wood on the floor appeared paper-thin. It would take a pretty penny to modernize the store without destroying the ambience. Walls would have to come down between existing stores on the block to allow for the volume the business needed to generate. There was a lot to do and the sooner they started the better. He had wasted enough time already.

The scent of the pumpkin soup wafted through the store. "What's that weird smell?" asked the landlord. Looking around he continued, "Place looks pretty good, considering the problems you had. They ever find out who broke the window?"

"No, the police haven't said anything yet," Olivia replied curtly, ignoring his first comment.

"Well, it makes me wonder what goes on in here, with people smashing fans and breaking windows. That kind of thing should only happen in a big city with drugs and things. Makes me wonder, ya know?" he said, nodding knowingly at Alex. Alex managed to be busy inspecting the brickwork as the landlord spoke.

Oliva bridled and was just opening her mouth to respond, when Dan stepped in.

"Mr. Hotchkiss, let's get back to the matter at hand. You said you were selling this building. Olivia has a lease until April. That gives her three months." Swinging around to Alex, he continued sarcastically, knowing the answer, "I don't suppose you'd extend the lease, now would you?"

Alex forced himself to look steadily into Olivia's eyes as he responded to Dan's question. "No. These buildings are to be renovated. No lease extensions will be allowed. As a matter of fact, tenants are going to be offered a buy-out for their last remaining months."

Olivia held the lock on his eyes, but her legs felt as dependable as wet noodles. With every fiber of her being fighting, she remained standing. "Then please take a look around on your own." Pulling Dan's hand, she led him back towards the kitchen. "I'm going to continue working, if you don't mind. Please shut the door on your way out."

Without another word, she walked into the kitchen, Dan in tow.

Chapter 18

Olivia took up the pen lying on top of her pumpkin soup recipe and began making notes on the paper. *Simmer chili and Thai basil in coconut milk before adding pumpkin.* Blindly, she walked over to the pot rack and grabbed another soup pan. She reached for the coconut milk, then stood frozen. Dan watched her silently, and took the pot out of her hand. "Somehow, this will be okay. Somehow, this will turn out to be the best thing for everyone. Trust me."

Olivia wanted to believe him. She really did. But right now, her world was crumbling around her again. She had not seen this coming. She had been so excited about her website and the cooking lessons. How had she been so blind?

Dan gently forced her to sit on the stool and brushed back a curl that had escaped from the scarf. Olivia's pale face remained immobile. From the front of the store, Alex took note of the gesture.

What seemed like an eternity later, Olivia got up and slowly began to clean up. "I'm going to put these things away and go home," she said slowly to no one in particular.

"I'll help," Dan said as he gathered the dirty dishes and headed towards the sink. Glancing out the kitchen door, he watched as the two men hunched down and examined the floorboards. Shaking his head, he continued to clean.

Olivia needed the solitude of her home. Dan didn't like it, but she refused to have him come over.

It was as though a funeral had just occurred and now she needed to be with her memories. Reality filtered through in a haze as she drove home. She had left Alex behind talking to the landlord. What did it matter? The store was no longer hers.

Chapter 19

Rays of pink tiptoed over the eastern horizon with the promise of a gentler day as Harry unlocked the back door to the store the next morning. The light sent a rosy glow through the front windows, but no aroma of coffee perked through the store. Bags of delivered bagels stood leaning un-opened outside against the front door. Harry racked his brain to try to remember if Olivia had mentioned something about not being here today. No! As a matter of fact, she was going to start filming. Maybe she just was late; but she was never late, and he was sure if something had happened she would've called. He heard Gilberta come in through the back.

"'Morning Sunshine," she sang out cheerily to him as she walked into the kitchen. The kitchen was dark and cold. No ovens warmed, and the buckets of prepared muffin batters remained in the reach-in refrigerator. Bewildered, she walked back out to the front where Harry worked on brewing coffee.

"Where's Olivia?" she asked.

"I don't know. I haven't seen or heard from her. This is weird. I'm worried."

"Did you call her house?"

"Not yet. I wanted to get some coffee going before calling. We open in half an hour and we're not going to be ready as it is. And I have to admit I was hoping she would come in or at least call."

"Here. I'll finish the coffee. You call," said Gilberta taking the filters out of Harry's hands.

Harry dialed the familiar number. He heard the phone ring interminably then finally go to voice mail. Olivia's cheery voice told him to leave a message, but he hung up instead. "She's not answering."

"Text her," urged Gilberta.

Harry took out his phone and sent the message and again there was no response.

Gilberta and Harry looked at each other worriedly. Something was wrong. "Listen, the store's going to open in a few minutes. Let's get the bakery together and I'll get the muffins in the oven. For one morning, customers are going to have to understand," said Gilberta, heading to the front door to bring in the bagels.

Silently, they went about their business as other staff began filtering in and getting to work. A pall hung over the store as though the life had been sucked out of it despite the sunshine pouring in. After the breakfast rush, Harry and Gilberta headed downstairs to call Olivia again. Still no answer.

In her bed, Olivia heard the phone ring. She buried herself under the quilt and put the pillow over her head. There was no one she wanted to talk to, nothing that mattered. And she was so tired; so tired she could sleep a week. Exhausted, she closed her eyes again and fell back into a troubled sleep.

At closing time, Harry locked the back door and turned to Gilberta. "Do you think we should call the police?"

"No. Not yet. Why don't we drive over to her house and see if we can see something?"

"Great idea. Let's go."

Twenty minutes later, the pair stood at Olivia's front door pounding the cast iron knocker against the wood below the stained glass window. Peering into the window next to the door, Harry could see nothing but cold darkness. " I don't think she's home," he said turning to Gilberta. "Now what?"

Gilberta's forehead crinkled in worry. "Something's not right. Maybe we should call the police."

"And say what? That our boss didn't show up for work today? What would they do?"

"I don't know, but I'm worried. What about all the crazy stuff that happened at the store? What if this is part of it?"

Harry exhaled. "Listen. I don't think we can call the police right now. Olivia just didn't show up for work today. What if she decided to take a day off?" Even to himself, he sounded unconvincing.

Gilberta looked back at the dark little stone house. It gave back no clues; no answers. "Okay. But if we don't hear from her, or see her by tomorrow morning I'm calling the police."

"Okay. I guess that's a plan."

The two drove back in silence to Gilberta's car in the store parking lot. "Try to get some sleep, Harry," she said as she got out of the car.

"You, too. See you in the morning. You know, I'm going to kill her if she just took the day off without saying anything to us." Harry threatened, secretly hoping that that would be the explanation.

Gilberta smiled wanly and slammed the door shut.

Chapter 20

Olivia heard a rhythmic pounding somewhere in the back of her mind. What song did it remind her of? It couldn't be too important if she couldn't remember. She buried more deeply under the quilts, rolled over and went back to sleep.

Chapter 21

She was suffocating and needed air. Somewhere there was something she needed to do, but she couldn't remember exactly what. With a groan, she opened her eyes and tried to orient herself. Quilts, sheets, and pillows piled on top of her, pressing down, making it difficult to breathe. With a shudder, she tore at the bedding, scrambling to get out from under the haze of dreamless sleep that had held her captive. Blearily, she looked for the alarm clock to see the time. 7:00 o'clock. Why had her alarm clock not gone off? She looked out the window and saw pitch black darkness. How could it be 7:00 o'clock when it was dark out? Sunrise was around 5:30am. Glancing around the room, she noticed the red light blinking on her answering machine. She must have really been asleep not to hear the phone ring. Confused, she went over and pushed the message button. Harry's voice, high pitched and anxious, was asking if he had forgotten whether she had told him that she would not be in the store today. Panic rose in her throat. She looked out the window again. What time was it? Grabbing her phone, she pressed Harry's number.

"Olivia! Where are you?" Harry answered, relief flooding through the phone.

"I'm home. Harry, what time is it?"

"It's 7:00 o'clock at night. Where have you been all day?"

Olivia glanced back at her bed. Was it possible she'd slept through an entire day? "I've been home. Harry, I think I slept all day..." Her voice trailed off. Slowly, she remembered Alex and Mr. Hotchkiss walking through her store as though she already was gone. Gone. Her store. Gone.

"Are you sick? Do you want me to come over? Gilberta and I came by and knocked on the door, but there was no answer. You must really have been asleep."

Olivia had a vague memory of the pounding. "I guess I really must have needed to sleep. Harry, can you come in a little early tomorrow morning? I need to talk to you."

Harry's stomach clenched. Something was going on. "Sure. I can come in at 6:00 instead of 6:30. Would that work?"

"Perfect. Thank you. And thank you for being such a good friend."

"You're welcome. I'm going to call Gilberta to let her know you are among the living. Geez. You really scared us, Olivia!"

"I'm sorry, Harry," Olivia said, touched that he had been so upset.

"It's okay. I'll see you in the morning. I'm just glad you're okay."

Olivia set the phone down. She heard her stomach grumble. Wryly, she realized she had not eaten in nearly twenty-four hours. Her mind was beginning to clear. She wrapped her bathrobe belt around her waist and slipped into her embroidered slippers. In the kitchen, she put the kettle on for tea and thoughtfully sautéed mushrooms with onions. Slowly, she constructed an omelet while reliving the scene of the previous day. Going through the motions of preparing good food calmed her and she was able to think about the situation with less panic. She sat down with a steaming cup of chamomile tea and willed herself to savor each bite. Looking out the window onto the dark old mansion, Olivia felt the flicker of a plan begin to percolate in her mind.

Chapter 22

Alex sat on the bed. The commitment papers for purchasing the buildings were all signed. His architect would fly in at the end of the week to take a look and begin preliminary proposals. He would fly back to Chicago next week and let his staff take over on the details. He should have been ecstatic. The price he was paying for the buildings was criminally cheap. Even if nothing were to come of this, the investment in real estate alone was worth it. So why was he awake at five a.m., unsettled and out of sorts? Buster rose from his place on the woven rug and rested his head in Alex's lap. "What's up old boy? Want to go for a walk? I know. I'm not very good company these days. Come on! Let's get back to normal." A few minutes later, Alex grabbed the dog's lead and headed out the door. Another crisp, rosy sunrise greeted them as they stepped onto the sidewalk. Looking around, Alex decided to head into town on Main St. since the sidewalks were clear and there were no people around yet to disturb his thoughts.

He walked through the quiet town, imagining it as his – his base of operations, his home. Olivia's face flashed into his thoughts. There it was – that yearning that intruded into all his dealings. He had seen Dan comfort her Sunday. He had felt her pain when Hotchkiss told her he was selling the store. Yet, this was the right business decision…and Olivia was not his to have. The memory of the kiss in her kitchen came back to haunt him. He knew he had felt her respond; the charge between them had been explosive. He wanted her. He wanted the flashing eyes, the soft ebony curls, and his hands on the curve of her back. He wanted her to want him just as badly. She wasn't married yet. There was room for a change in course, wasn't there? He would give her a generous settlement for her store, then he would ask her to come on board with European Gourmet. How could she refuse? Together they would conquer the world! Nothing would stop them. It was the perfect solution. His excitement rose with each step, the sun shining in reflection of his mood. This could be his town. No, this would be his home.

    Looking up from his thoughts, he realized he was standing in front of Sweet Sage. The store was dark with no movement inside. A white van pulled up in front of the store just as Buster made movements towards a planter, indicating a need. Alex tugged him away and stopped in front of the store. A young man jumped out and opened the back gate to pull out two large bags filled with warm bagels. He placed the bags against the front door. "They don't open for another hour," he informed Alex as got back into the van. Buster pulled at the leash as the van pulled away. A tree was conveniently waiting nearby for him to do his business.

    Alex realized that in his fog this morning, he had forgotten to take along a bag with which to clean up after Buster. Glancing at the bags by the door, he wondered if he could tear off a small piece big enough to scoop up Buster's business and throw it in the trash can. He walked over and was just about to tear off a piece when the lights inside the store snapped on. Alex looked up with a jolt, then thought that whoever was there might be able to give him something a little handier to clean up the mess. And, if it was Olivia…he smiled. He was about to turn her life around.

Olivia snapped the lights on. She felt good about her plans, but still mourned the loss of this treasured store. She headed to the front door to bring in the daily delivery of bagels. Someone was standing there with his back to the door, looking across the street. The store hours were clearly marked on the front door. Suddenly, she recognized the big dog standing by the person. She caught her breath sharply, anger coursing through her. Alex turned around to see her face freeze into a stony mask. She unlocked the door and reached for the bags. "What are you doing here? It's still my store – at least for a little while."

"Absolutely. Buster and I went for a walk this morning and unfortunately he had to take care of business and I forgot to take anything along to clean up. Do you by any chance have a small bag I could use?"

Olivia glanced at Buster, who stood there smiling at her with his foolish grin. With a sigh she said, "Come in. Let the Health Department come, if they want."

Alex grabbed one of the bags and carried it inside, laying it on the large glass counter. "Do you really go through this many bagels in a day?"

"Yes," she replied curtly.

"Listen. Do you have a minute to talk? I want to apologize for Hotchkiss on Sunday and I want to talk with you about an idea I had."

Olivia looked into the silvery blue eyes of the man standing before her. She had driven in this morning clear-headed, ready for the next phase of her life. It did not involve this man who had the annoying ability to send the blood coursing through her veins faster than anyone yet. And she hated him. Glancing at the clock she said, "I have fifteen minutes before Harry comes in for a meeting, so talk fast."

"First of all, you should know that you will receive a generous compensation for leaving the premises ahead of schedule, if you agree to do so. Secondly, there is no reason why you can't be part of my business. I would like to offer you a position with European Gourmet. You can tailor it to your needs. You know the clientele in town better than anyone else. You could run the catering business however you wanted to do it. It would be a win-win situation."

Olivia had been busy laying the bagels out on trays according to flavor. Her eyes focused squarely on what she was doing. How dare this arrogant and self-satisfied man take her store away from her and then try to buy her! She didn't need him. If anything, he was going to end up needing her. She deliberately put the tray into the bakery case before looking up.

"I might take the settlement, if it's the right amount and depending on the date set to vacate, but I am certainly not going to join European Gourmet." Her eyes flashed in anger as she continued, "How dare you think you can manipulate me so easily. I'll be fine; no, I'll be more than fine. Now I suggest you leave to figure out your generous settlement and leave me to run my business while I still have it."

Alex stood still. Buster tugged at the leash looking meaningfully at the door. They heard the back door click open and footsteps heralded the arrival of Harry. He stopped. Surprise and puzzlement crossed his face as he surveyed the scene. Olivia glowered at a stony-faced Alex who was holding on to a leash that was attached to what looked like a small horse. He checked his watch. Quarter to six. A little early for the drama to start. His already anxious stomach clenched a little tighter.

Olivia looked back to Harry. "Thanks for coming in early, Harry. Mr. Dumaurier was just leaving." She walked meaningfully to the front door and held it open. Buster, in his usual enthusiastic manner, lunged for the door pulling Alex behind him.

"My office will be in touch about the settlement," he managed to utter coldly as the door swung closed behind him. Only after the door slammed closed did he remember that he had business to deal with. And no way, now, to deal with it.

Olivia watched him walk away stiffly. What had she just done? Could that have been the way to go? She looked back at Harry who was looking at her questioningly. No. She was going to do it her way. No one was going to own her.

Chapter 23

Olivia turned to Harry. "I didn't expect him with the bagels this morning," she commented wryly.

"What did he want?" asked Harry.

Olivia looked at Harry. "Help me finish setting up breakfast and I'll tell you everything."

Over the course of the next hour, Olivia filled Harry in on the loss of the store and began to outline some of her ideas on how to go forward with her dream. It was risky, but so had starting this business been chancy...and look where they were today. Sort of...

Olivia sighed.

By the time Gilberta and Lena walked through the door, Harry's head was spinning. No wonder Olivia slept all of yesterday. He felt like he needed a nap already.

Olivia looked at him and said, "Harry, I don't think I want everyone to know everything yet. Could you do me a big favor and not speak to anyone about this? Not even John?"

"I promise. But we're going to have to say something pretty soon. These people have jobs they depend on, and this is going to freak them out!"

"I know. But I'd like to tell them calmly and not at the beginning of the day. I'll set up a family meeting and talk to everybody about it then. Agreed?"

Harry looked at her. He had always trusted Olivia. If anyone could pull them out of the weeds, she could. "Agreed."

All of a sudden, Olivia's eyes opened wide and she exclaimed, "Harry! Claire! Her daughter's wedding! You know she's going to hear about this. She'll be panicked. If I were her, I'd want someone else more stable involved! I have to call her!"

"Well, it's a little early to do that right now. Maybe you should wait until after the breakfast rush."

With a suggestion of a smile on the corner of her lips, Olivia said, "You're right. Okay, I'll wait. And remember, nothing to anyone."

"My lips are sealed."

Chapter 24

The months flew by in the blink of an eye. The settlement had been generous and Claire had been so incensed at the news of the take-over that she promised to go to Town Hall and make a fuss over every little item regarding European Gourmet. She, at least, could make their life miserable, and true to her words, she had. She was fully confident that with her daughter's wedding just on the horizon, Olivia had it well under control.

Though the time had flown by, it had been excruciating for Olivia and Harry to let go all the staff and oversee the removal of all the equipment. Olivia's heart had felt like it was breaking the day she turned the key on the door for the last time. The only thing that kept depression at bay was knowing that a new chapter was opening in front of her.

Five months later, Olivia sat at her old desk placed in front of the window in her second-floor office overlooking the lawn that ran towards her little cottage. The snow was long gone and tulips cheerily lined the circular drive in front of the mansion. She heard the workers putting the final touches on the kitchen downstairs. The health inspector was due in an hour to give the final blessing on the project. The settlement from European Gourmet had been generous enough to allow her to put a down payment on the mansion and begin renovations. Income from the website had allowed her to keep Harry, Gilberta, and Marta on the payroll. The store's closing had been heart-wrenchingly sad, but Sweet Sage's website, her guest appearances on local cable cooking shows, and her food articles in the local newspapers had kept her customers aware of her and anxiously awaiting the grand opening of her new enterprise. The cooking school and catering company would open its doors in two weeks, barring any last minute problems. If all went as planned, the gardens would be constructed within the month, with a fulltime gardener in place to keep it producing the greens and herbs necessary for her recipes. Olivia smiled. Dan had said that losing the store might be for the best and that everything would turn out well, and so far, it had. There had been no more crazy incidences such as broken windows, even though the police had never found the culprit. European Gourmet was in the middle of a massive renovation of the entire block and it did not look like they were going to be ready for business any time soon. But most importantly, she had come into her own writing cookbooks, getting the cooking school ready, and learning how to videotape classes for her website. Gilberta, Marta, and Harry had been indispensable. And here she was, in her beloved mansion, safe from the vagaries and whims of other people; no landlord, no menacing corporation to take her down. True, it still needed a massive amount of work, but the business spaces downstairs were ready to go – as long as they passed inspection, she thought wryly. Footsteps up the stairs brought her out of her reverie.

"Well, Captain, looks like we're as ready as we're ever going to be. Let them bring on the inspectors!" smiled Harry.

"Sometimes I feel like I am dreaming. If someone had predicted this would happen a year ago, I would have thought they were crazy."

Harry looked thoughtful. "It does seem like a lifetime away now. So much has happened. I feel like we've moved mountains in the last couple of months. Getting ready for one wedding is going to be a cinch in comparison. Even if the inspector finds something today, we've got six weeks before we need to actually start cooking."

Olivia smiled. Harry looked calmer and more content than he had since she met him. It had been hard to lay off the staff when the store closed in February. Harry's soft heart had nearly broken as he said goodbye to Lena and the others. But hard work and a burgeoning relationship with someone who actually appeared to be decent brought back the smiles and sarcastic wit she had come to treasure.

"Well, let's hope the inspection doesn't take too long this afternoon. I'd like to get the shoot for the next video class finished today. If we get started right after she leaves, we might be finished by five. That way Marta can load it onto the web tomorrow."

"The proofs for the cookbook were delivered this morning. Want me to go over it with Gilberta while we're waiting?"

"That would be great. Are we ready for tomorrow's Channel 8 show? I was waiting for the nopales to be delivered. Have you seen them come in?"

"I just checked them in," said Gilberta as she walked in the door. "We're all set."

The three friends looked at each other. "Who would have believed that we would be here four months ago?" asked Gilberta.

"It is remarkable. And we thought we were doing well with the store. It's almost as though having the store was holding us back. I guess the web is just that much more powerful, never mind television," reflected Olivia. "And here I thought my life was over when European Gourmet came to town!"

"You have to admit that was not pretty. The only reason we're here is because you have fantastic ideas. Not everyone could have rescued a business like this!" Harry noted.

A sense of contentment washed over Olivia. Life was full and satisfying right now. Everything was perfect. "We make a good team."

As Olivia looked out the window, a red Toyota pulled into the circular driveway in front of the mansion's majestic front pillars. The passenger window opened and she saw something get thrown out towards the house. Immediately the car sped away. "Hey! Did you see that?"

Harry leaned over the desk and watched the red Toyota speed down the road. His face blanched visibly. "That looked like Tommy's car again. What the hell…!?!"

He bolted downstairs and flung open the door to find what looked like a crudely made smoke bomb smoking under the hydrangea bush beneath the new kitchen window. At least he thought it was a smoke bomb. "Hey, bring a bucket of water! Fast!" he yelled back.

Olivia and Gilberta, who had been flying down the stairs on his heels, made abrupt turns into the kitchen. Olivia yanked a large stockpot from the pot rack, dragged it over to the industrial sink. Gilberta turned both faucets on full blast and used the hose to fill the pot. Together they grabbed the handles and sloshed it to where Harry was pointing to a smoking ball under the low branches. The water cascaded over the device, drowning any smoke that remained.

"I'm calling the police. He's not getting away with it this time," vowed Harry. "I knew he was mad about my going out with John, but I didn't think he was crazy enough to do those kinds of things. I'm sure he's the one who wrecked the store last December."

"What makes you so sure it was Tommy?" asked Olivia.

"I thought it was him before, but I wasn't sure, so I didn't say anything, but I should have. This time, I'm sure. I broke up with him because he was too weird. Now, he's just a rat…and dangerous."

"Okay. Let's call and get this over with." With a sigh, Olivia led them into the kitchen where Harry made the call and she and Gilberta mopped up the spilled water. Well, almost everything was perfect, thought Olivia.

Chapter 25

Alex flew back in from Chicago to inspect the work on the buildings. It had been three long months and work was progressing more slowly than he had anticipated. At every turn, it seemed Town Hall had another question or inspection to perform.

He had stayed in town and watched as Olivia closed her store and moved out. Pangs of guilt had actually assailed him, though he felt the settlement had been more than generous. He didn't know whether it was her stubborn refusal to join him or watching her close the store that bothered him the most. His perfect dream of working with her and conquering the world together had been shot down ferociously. In any case, it was easier to fly out and manage from Chicago than to stay. He had hired a seasoned crew to transform the row of stores. It was easy to convince himself that he was needed at the helm in Chicago…where his real home was. Overall, corporate sales were still soft and had not rebounded from the weak economy. This new project took revenue, but he believed it was the key the company needed to boost it back into the kind of profitability it had enjoyed just three years earlier.

Alex drove into the parking lot behind the newly renovated block of stores that now sported the iconic deep blue and red trim of European Gourmet. Utility trucks still filled the spaces near the main entrance. He parked next to the electrician and entered through the quietly gliding doors. He nodded to himself in approval. The customer experience started at the door. Looking in, the old wooden and brick walls were still there, but everything else had changed. Sleek modern lighting showcased the modern shelving and glass food cases. What was left of Olivia's warm store was transformed into a modern emporium with an old-world charm. He felt his cell phone vibrate as he crossed the floor. His uncle. For a moment he was tempted not to answer. Resignedly, he tapped the screen. "Hello, Leo. What do you have for me?"

"Alex! Glad you're back in town, boy. Have you had a chance to read the local paper yet, or look at the local channel? No? Well, take a look. That little chippy you sent on her way is making headlines. Might be worth keeping an eye on. Now, I'm not saying she could cause trouble, but she's on to something. Might behoove you to take a look."

"Leo, what the hell are you talking about?"

"That girl with the curly hair you took the store from – she's beginning to make a name for herself around here with her newspaper column, and she's a mighty fine sight on the squawk box. Rumor has it, she's about to open a big catering business and cooking school in that old mansion…which you so foolishly refused to buy, I might add. Big mistake letting go that property."

Alex appeared to be watching the electricians work as his uncle spoke, but it was the memory of Olivia's soft lips passionately responding to his that captured his thoughts. It did not surprise him that

Olivia would make a name for herself on television. Who wouldn't fall for that face? So being in Chicago all this time had erased the intensity of his longing? He was a fool. And now he might have another kind of problem to deal with.

"Alex, you there? Did you hear me?"

"Hm? Yes. I heard you. I'll look into it."

"Look into what? You didn't hear a word I said, did you? Listen, I'm going out to dinner tonight with some of my staff. Why don't you join us over at The Black Goose Grill, say around seven? Maybe you'll talk sense then."

The last thing Alex wanted to do was go out to dinner and watch his uncle get drunk with members of his firm. But... he had no excuse. "Sure. I'll be there. See you later."

Across town, Dan sat in his sleek office finishing the last note on a brief. His thoughts were disturbed by the ringing of the phone. Leo. What could he want at this late hour? "Hello, Leo."

"Dan!" came the hearty voice. "A few of the boys and I are going out to The Black Goose for a quick one after work. You'll join us, of course," Leo's voice rang with no expectation of being refused.

Dan sighed. "Sure. I have a few more things to catch up on. What time will you be there?"

"Sevenish. Good. See you there." And he hung up.

Dan looked at the phone in his hand. He was comfortable here at the firm. Maybe too comfortable.

He went back to his work with a worm of anger beginning to burrow.

What seemed like only a short time later, Dan looked at his watch and realized it was way past seven. "Oh hell…" With a sigh, he put away his papers and headed over to the Grill. All he wanted to do was go home, have a drink, and read the day's newspaper. Listening to Leo spout on about some inane topic was almost more than he could bear. But, here he was…He opened the back door of the restaurant door and walked in.

Just a mile away, Alex entered his hotel room from having walked Buster. "Okay old boy, I need to go out. Hold down the fort," he said, scratching him behind his ears. Buster obediently lay on the floor with his paws crossed in front of him, his eyes adoringly fixed on Alex's face. Alex smiled. This was one uncomplicated part of his life. Buster loved him and he loved Buster. End of story. "Yah, me, too," he said with a final scratch as he rose to get ready to leave. Alex decided to walk over to the restaurant since it was not far. Sooner than he wished, he found himself at the front door of the Black Goose. He opened the door and was immediately assaulted by loud braying laughter emanating from the bar. He nearly turned on his heels, when the door at the far side of the corridor opened and Dan walked in.

"Alex! I didn't know you were in town." Dan walked toward Alex with his hand outstretched. The animosity he had felt towards him had begun to dissipate as Olivia's new life began to take shape successfully, though wariness remained. This man was capable of anything, and Olivia's newfound success was just that...new.

Alex's shoulders stiffened and his shake was perfunctorily courteous. He would have to get used to meeting up with Dan and Olivia in this small town. He was just going to have to be a big boy about it.

"Dan," he nodded. "How are you?"

"Fine."

A strained silence fell between the two of them. Ironically, both welcomed the sudden appearance of Leo, who had just stepped out of the bar, heading to the men's room.

"Well, well, well! Look who's here! My two favorite boys!" Putting his arms around their shoulders, he shepherded them towards the bar. "Go on in. I'll meet up with you in a minute. Got to take care of business, you know!" he winked as he headed to the men's room.

Dan and Alex edged their way into the crowded room and headed over to the bar. As they waited for their order, Alex turned to Dan. This was the time to show he was a big boy, at least to himself. "So I hear your girlfriend is about to open up a cooking school in the Meres property. I'm sorry she didn't take my offer to come on board. We could use someone like her in the company, but it looks like she landed on her feet. Will she be joining you tonight?"''

Dan looked at Alex, confused. Maybe he didn't hear right in all the noise. Did he still think Olivia was his girlfriend? And what did it matter if he did? Dan sighed. He couldn't live with a guilty conscience, for any reason…even if he didn't like what the guy had done to his best friend. "Are you talking about Olivia?"

"Yes. How is she doing?"

"Listen, I need to clear one thing up. She's not my girlfriend."

It was Alex's turn to be confused. Had he heard clearly? Just as he was going to ask for clarification, a hand slapped his back. Unfortunately, Leo was back from taking care of business.

"Come on, boys. Get your drinks and let's go back here where we can hear one another," he said as the bartender handed Dan and Alex their drinks.

Maneuvering through the crowd, they headed towards the only table with open seats in the back of the room. A young woman sat at the table guarding a coat. She rose as they approached. Dan smiled to her. He had not seen much of her since she had come to his holiday party on Robert's arm.

"Tiffany! Nice to see you here. Mind if we have a seat?" asked Leo.

"Please do. I'm sure Nicole won't mind."

"Nicole! Our new office manager? Didn't know you two were friendly."

"We're just getting to know each other, but she's great," Tiffany responded shyly.

"Well, that's nice. Is Robert here somewhere?"

"I wouldn't know." Tiffany said, smiling shyly at Dan.

Dan grinned back.

Alex noted the exchange with some confusion. Dan neatly maneuvered to take the seat next to her, forcing Leo to sit to his left... leaving Alex to sit on the other side of the seat with the coat. He watched Dan chatting with Tiffany. It was only too obvious that he was enjoying her company. What had transpired between Olivia and Dan while he was away?

Leo leaned over and bellowed in his ear, "So? Did you get a copy of the paper? That girl you bought the store from, what's her name, has a big spread in the Living section. And, here, take a look at this," he said pulling out his phone. "She's got this website that has videos on how to make things. It brings up market lists, how much it costs, and all the fancy nutrition information that everybody's talking about."

Alex took the phone away from his uncle. How could he have missed this? Why hadn't his staff kept up with the competition? The site also boasted several pages such as a marketplace to buy hard-to-find items and sample catering menus complete with photos. A note on the front page heralded the grand opening of the catering business and cooking school in two weeks. Alex didn't know whether to smile or be angry. So, Olivia was able to continue her business. She was going to give his catering department stiff competition, he thought grimly. This is the stuff his company should be doing. Why weren't they? Despite his anger, it was her face he couldn't stop watching. In one video, she was deftly teaching how to quickly debone a chicken with gravity, yet with a smile in her voice. Her dark curls were caught up in a colorful scarf with one tendril obstinately escaping. Damn his traitorous body! He was sure that what he was feeling was a completely physical reaction. It had been a long time since he had held someone in his arms.

A shapely young woman holding a wine glass came over to the table and pulled out the chair with the coat. "Hi, Mr. Barbier," she said cheerily. "I was busy listening to everyone's suggestions on how to run the office, or I would have been back sooner. Lawyers certainly do have strong opinions that they don't mind sharing," she laughed.

"I guess it's a good thing they didn't eat you alive," joked Leo. "Didn't I tell you, the last office manager was made into mincemeat and eaten up at Christmas!"

Everyone groaned.

"Nicole, let me introduce you to my nephew Alex. He's running that big new renovation downtown."

Alex politely shook her hand. "Nice to meet you. I hope my uncle is not abusing you too badly at work with his sense of humor. It can be deadly."

Nicole smiled flirtatiously at Alex, an obvious invitation in her eyes. "So far, so good."

Alex still had the phone in his hand. He glanced at Olivia's face a final time before sliding the screen off. He returned the phone to his uncle and looked back at Nicole with a smile.

Chapter 26

Olivia sat contentedly in her worn jeans and thick heather green sweater on a stool at the large stainless steel worktable in the new catering kitchen. A cheery red ribbon captured her unruly curls, lending her the air of a schoolgirl. The work in the mansion was done for the moment and life had taken on a comfortable rhythm. Her hand rested gently around a cerulean blue mug of steaming coffee as she edited the proofs for her cookbook. The photographer had done a lovely job of capturing the colors and textures of the dishes. It had taken time to test all the recipes, but now they all worked. She smiled thinking of Dan and his friends good naturedly testing six versions of the same braised rosemary chicken with lemon and olives. They had gamely written notes on the dishes which she took back to finalize the recipes. Olivia took a sip of coffee and began the process of checking the pages. Deep in thought, she did not hear the footsteps entering behind her.

Alex had parked his black BMW in the front circular drive of the mansion he had almost owned for a few days and, on trying the front door, found that it opened readily. He entered and walked down the warm saffron tinted front hall, noticing an open door leading off to the left. The thought of calling out and announcing himself crossed his mind, but something held him back. He advanced towards the door, then froze. He found himself gazing across a sparkling white walled kitchen anchored by a brick red tile floor. Stainless steel appliances shone in the sunshine coming from a large window. A curly haired figure sat on a stool at one of the steel tables, deeply absorbed in her work. A white apron hugged her shapely waist, and tendrils escaped unnoticed down her neck. His hands ached with the desire to caress the curls and wrap themselves around her waist. Apparently last night with Nicole had not tamed his desires.

Get a grip, old man, he scolded himself wryly. He coughed lightly and said coolly, "May I interrupt your work?"

Olivia jumped and spun around. "You could have knocked..." Her voice trailed off as she realized who was standing there. "What do you want?" she asked coldly.

"I heard all about your new enterprise and thought I would come and check out the competition."

"Why? So you can pull this out from under me, too? You have some nerve. Luckily, this time I don't think you have any control over me."

"No. I simply came to look. And perhaps see if we could work together, instead of against each other."

"You've got to be kidding! After what you did to me? Really? Why would I even think of working with you? I can't trust you worth a damn."

Alex winced. Okay. He deserved that. "Business is business. If I hadn't bought the building, someone else would have. Your landlord was desperate, let's not forget."

"True, but someone else might not have kicked me out. Maybe they would have just continued the lease. You came in, kicked us out, and put in your huge competitor. After telling me you would never hurt me!" Olivia's cheeks flamed pink as she uttered that last sentence, her body flooding with a ghost of the heat that had burned between them in that one long ago kiss.

Alex, noting the rosy cheeks, took a deep breath. His own unruly emotions made it difficult for his mind to think rationally. *What had he been thinking, coming here this morning?*

"I'm serious about the offer to work together. With your savvy and my business expertise, the sky's the limit. I know your store is gone, but I'm almost thinking I did you a favor…"

"Get out!" Olivia exploded, her finger jabbing at Alex's business-suited chest emphasizing each word she spoke. "Get out right now! You did not do me a favor. I was working on these ideas the day you came into the store to look at it with Hotchkiss. What do you think I was doing there? Losing my store set me back months and forced me to fire dear friends who depended on me for their jobs." Her fingers jabbed even more roughly now, forcing Alex to step backwards with each jab. "You…did…not…do…me…a…favor! You are a self-centered, egotistical man. Stay out of my life and leave me alone!"

By this time, Alex found himself back out in the hallway. He put his hands up in surrender. "I'm sorry to have been the one to cause the pain. I still maintain that it was going to happen, sooner rather than later. I wish you all the best." He turned on his heel and strode to his car. This had been a colossal mistake. What had given him the idea that Olivia would have entertained the idea of merging with his business, anyway? When would he stop thinking about working with her? Another instance of thinking with his emotions rather than his brains. Disgusted, he drove off to review grand opening plans with the staff.

Olivia stood trembling at the kitchen door watching as Alex disappeared. What had just happened? What was that crazy reaction she just had? Was it Alex hurting her that she feared? Alex couldn't hurt her. If anything, she could cause real trouble for him. She had the town eating out of her hands. The catering event orders already were tremendous, with almost every weekend booked between now and October. So…what about Alex fired her blood and made her heart race? Unbidden, that damned kiss intruded, once again, into her thoughts. She was still haunted by something that had taken place in the space of a moment. And even Alex nearly putting her out of business couldn't wipe it away.

Returning to her stool, she found it hard to concentrate on the book proofs. The same recipe had flashed by her eyes for the third time when the phone rang. She looked at the caller id. Food. What was "Food"? Probably someone selling a magazine subscription.

"Hello?"

"Ms. Caron?" asked a clipped voice.

"Yes?"

"This is Cassie Douglass from the Food Channel. We've been watching your local cable show and were interested in talking to you about a concept we had in mind. Could you come down to New York next week to meet with our staff?"

Olivia's jaw dropped nearly to the floor. Things were happening way too quickly today. "What type of concept do you have in mind?" she managed to croak.

"Very much what you are doing – flavorful, quick, and healthy. We need talent that understands the camera, can produce what the consumer wants, and as a bonus, is attractive. Are you interested?"

Olivia cringed at the last condition. She did not like looking at herself in the mirror and spent almost no time fussing with her looks. What you saw was what you got. As for being comfortable with a camera, the cable show had swept away any butterflies she might have had, and after having watched the camera operators in action, she understood what needed to happen. "Yes, I'm interested. When and where is this next week?" she forced herself to say calmly.

"Great. You'll be meeting with our production team on Monday at two pm at the

Woolworth Tower in Manhattan. A staff person will be contacting you on more of the specifics a little later. See you then."

"See you then," echoed Olivia.

She pinched herself to make sure she was awake. She was. Slowly, a big grin spread across her face. No, she did not need Alex or European Gourmet. Ironically, she privately suspected Alex was right, that he had done her a favor by forcing her out of the store. Would she have had the time to devote to the cable show and website if she had had to take care of the store, too? Maybe not. Ruefully, she remembered her poking finger, her vitriolic speech, and the dismay on Alex's face. But, damn it! He did force her out of the store! What if she had not landed on her feet? Why was she even giving him the time of day? Because of that ill-considered kiss? Was she that desperate and needy? The smile slid off her face. She infuriated herself. That damned man kept popping into her life and her thoughts in the most obnoxious way. She didn't need him. She didn't want him. She wished he would disappear completely from her life and mind. She did not need anyone other than herself and her friends. She sighed.

Harry walked through the kitchen door just as Olivia decided she was insane.

"Get a grip!" she commanded herself.

"Well, hello to you, too," responded Harry, "Anything I can help you with?"

"Oh, Harry! You won't believe what just happened!

"Okay. Try me."

"Well, first, Alex Dumaurier paid a surprise visit."

"What!" interrupted Harry. "The nerve of that man!" All of a sudden, Harry's eyes widened in horror. "He can't do anything to us, can he?"

"No, no. Don't worry, he can't. At this point, I think he needs us more than we need him. He actually was starting to propose working together when I forced him out."

Olivia grew quiet. Harry looked into the dark eyes that suddenly seemed so far away. "You're not actually thinking of doing that… are you?" he asked with a worried frown.

"Of course not! It's just that…"her voice trailed off.

"It's just that what? That guy almost ruined your life, and let's not forget poor Lena. Until we were able to hire her back, she had it rough!"

"You're right. But, that's not what I was thinking about."

"Then what, for goodness sake!"

She smiled impishly at her friend. "He's sexy."

"Oh, girl! Is that what this is all about? You know there are other fish in the ocean, right? I could fix you up in two shakes of your curly head!"

"Hmmm. But you have to admit he has a certain je ne sais quoi to him, don't you?"

Harry sighed. Of all the men Olivia could be attracted to. Maybe she just had not had someone for too long. He decided then and there to fix her up and force her to go out on a date. "I think you have been working too hard. It's time to play a little bit."

"Well, let me tell you what happened next. We may not have that much time to play. The Food Channel called and wants to meet with me next week about a show. They saw me on our cable show and want to do something similar."

Harry let out a hoot loud enough to be heard in the back garden. He grabbed Olivia's hands and swung her off the stool. "You're going to be famous!" he crowed exuberantly spinning her around.

Olivia laughed, "Stop! Stop. I'm getting dizzy!"

"You think you're dizzy now, wait until you start working on a show! Life will really be dizzy then!"

"I hope not. I don't want the show to take over the whole business. We have something really special here and we have to keep it strong. Speaking of which, we need to finish these proofs and get ready to film tomorrow."

"Work, work, work," Harry smiled. "Alright. Move over and I'll take the next chapter."

Chapter 27

The late afternoon summer sun sent shards of light streaming through the architectural blinds in the second story office to punctuate the numbers on the pages Alex held in his hands. The broken pattern of sun accentuated the sharp planes in Alex's face as he grimly studied the report. Although the new flagship store had gotten good reviews, sales were soft, and the other stores remained slow as well. The hope that this store would lift all the others in the wake of its success did not appear to be happening. Something needed to change. Competition from Sweet Sage was eating away a bigger chunk of the business than he ever would have anticipated. European Gourmet would need a hell of a holiday season to make up for lost revenues. He threw the report onto the desk, grabbed his coffee mug, and headed downstairs to the sales floor. Maybe a quick walk and a jolt of caffeine would waken inspiration.

The store, spacious now in its expanded form, had a golden air to it, but only a few customers roamed throughout. Alex stepped over to the wooden coffee bar surrounded by shelves of cookbooks and culinary magazines. As he waited for the barista to fill his mug, he glanced over to the magazine rack where his eyes locked onto the smiling eyes of Olivia holding a basket full of fresh garden produce. Red hot frustration swept through him like a firestorm. This woman…was at the core of everything he desired, needed. Anger displaced the frustration.

Anger at himself for being outwitted by a single young woman; anger at his hunger for her.

"Mr. Dumaurier? Sir, here's your coffee," the barista said timidly a second time as he slid Alex's mug to him.

Alex took the mug with a curt nod and headed back upstairs to his office. He was going to do something about this once and for all. His sanity and the health of the store depended on it.

Chapter 28

Oblivious to the turmoil she was causing five miles away, Olivia sat in her office poring over all the reports. Her accountant had just completed the first quarter returns and the numbers were glorious. With a sigh, she set the reports down and looked out the window. The sun shone brightly on the yellow, pink, and blue beds of lupines, snapdragons, and cosmos dancing in the breeze in front of the mansion. Life was good, but running into the city two days a week for the show and managing her business was beginning to sap her creativity. The sun called to her. Unable to resist, she walked downstairs and out the back door to the kitchen garden. Jonathon, the young university student who managed the gardens between classes, waved as she approached.

"Hey, stranger. Long time no see," he grinned, reaching down to snap a fresh pea pod off a vine. "Where you been?" he asked handing her the pea pod.

Olivia bit into the crisp green pod, savoring its warm earthy sweetness. "In New York and in my office," she replied dejectedly. "I should be up there now, but I heard the garden calling."

Jonathon nodded. "I wish I could help take some of the load off your shoulders, but I don't think I'd be any good in the office."

"You are exactly where you should be and you're working miracles. The grounds look gorgeous and the vegetables are superb. Don't even think about changing anything."

"Aye, aye, Captain, "he laughed.

With a sigh, Olivia popped the rest of the pea pod into her mouth and headed back up to the office. It was not that she didn't like doing the show, and she was certainly ecstatic over how well the business was running, but even with Harry and Gilberta, there was too much to do. Happily, they had been able to hire back many of the staff they had had to let go when the store closed. Harry was especially happy to have Lena back on the catering staff and organizing the cooking school. No, what she needed was a clone of herself to take on the mundane business chores that were so necessary, yet took her time away from doing what she loved...creating. Olivia daydreamed about having a clone to hand off her unwanted responsibilities and laughed. The laughter died on her lips as she realized she may have just come up with the answer to her problems. She could hire a responsible and knowledgeable business manager. In fact, the business might run even more smoothly that it did now with the right person in place. Excitement bubbled up inside her. It would be wonderful to be able to focus on the recipes, the writing, and the shows again with no paperwork waiting for her when she came home. But, who could she trust to take care of her baby the way she did? Diane, her old bookkeeper came to mind, but Olivia knew that that was all she was, a good bookkeeper. She needed something more; someone who could really take control.

Back in the office, she looked at the papers blindly and decided she needed a real break. Everything could wait till tomorrow. She glanced out the window and realized she needed to talk her ideas out with someone other than Harry or Gilberta. Dan might be able to help her think this through. She smiled thinking of Dan. Unbelievably, he had begun dating Tiffany, the young woman from his office. Though she was young, she was sweet, and despite first appearances, had a good head on her shoulders. Dan finally seemed to have found someone to love him the way he needed to be loved. His relationship with Tiffany had made him a little scarce, but she had been so busy that she hardly noticed. She called him now, hoping that he was free.

"Hi, Dan! Do you have time to spare for an old friend who needs advice?"

"Olivia! Of course I do! Tiffany and I were just going to barbecue something simple on the grill tonight. Would you like to join us, or is this something more serious?"

Olivia felt a twinge of some unidentified emotion as she heard Dan's cheery words. Was it possible she was jealous that her best friend was no longer solely devoted to her and at her every beck and call? She straightened up in her chair and said, "I would love to. That sounds perfect. I do want to ask you something about the business if you don't mind."

"I don't mind and I'm sure it's fine with Tiffany, if it's not too confidential."

"It's not that private. Tiffany just might be bored!" she laughed. "What time should I come by, and what can I bring?"

"Come by at seven and just bring yourself. Tiffany will be totally panicked to hear that the great chef is coming over for dinner, but hopefully a glass of wine will calm her down," he laughed.

"Aha! I'll have to bring a good bottle, then! Seven it is and please let Tiffany know that I love having other people do the cooking!"

She hung up the phone and recalled all the times she had been the one to cook on Dan's barbecue or in his kitchen; all the heart-to-heart talks they'd had since Michael died. Now another woman was there to give him what he craved. Something that she had been unable to give him.

Despite the golden afternoon sun peeking through the office window, a shadow fell over Olivia's face. She ached for the love and trust she had had with Michael all those years ago. Alex's steely gray eyes flashed through her thoughts. There was physical attraction there, she grudgingly admitted, but trust was another thing altogether. Longing and loneliness coursed through her. The rosy light coming through the window nudged at Olivia. With a sigh, she closed the computer, put the papers away, and walked out the back to the trail leading to the park. Maybe a walk through the woods would help clear her mind. She looked down at her espadrilles.

The trail was pretty well groomed and she wasn't going to go that far. They would do.

It was lovely out there - soft, verdant, and deliciously fragrant. The scent of damp earth swirled with the honeysuckle in bloom. Step by step, she could feel herself relaxing. Her shoulders loosened with each stride. Her mind began to empty itself of the tension stored inside from days of hard work.

She had gone a little more than half an hour on the trail when a crashing in the underbrush disturbed her peace. Startled, she stopped and listened. The sound was heading her way, she was sure. Olivia froze - then madly, looked around for a weapon. A broken branch lay nearby. Quickly she grabbed it and stood still. Trying to quell her panic, she ran through the possibilities. There were no bears or mountain lions in these woods, as far as she knew. If it were a dog, she would stay still and try to protect herself. She took her phone out. The least she could do was call 911. Quickly she punched in the numbers but did not press send. Phone in one hand, thumb poised on send, the branch in the other, she prepared herself for the onslaught.

A final crash and out of the brush leapt a giant black dog sporting a huge sloppy grin. Instantly, Olivia recognized the grin. Buster! Laughing in relief, she dropped the branch and readied herself for the affectionate greeting.

Buster danced around her maniacally, then stood on his hind legs to put his paws on her shoulders. Prepared this time, Olivia was able to withstand the onslaught of affection.

"Down, boy. You're a good boy. Down...down..." she said gently, holding his paws and directing him back towards the ground. She scratched him behind the ears as he licked her under her chin. Her smile faltered as it occurred to her that he could not possibly be alone in the woods – unless he somehow had run far, far away. Quickly she scanned the area, but no other human appeared. "How did you get here? Did you escape a horrible prison somewhere?" she asked him, ruffling the fur around his ears. With a slobbering grin, he responded with a wet lick to her nose. "Hey! That's enough. Okay. Come on. I'm going for a walk and you might as well join me." Standing, she looked for a leash, but did not find one. "Well, I guess I'm going to have to trust that you will walk by my side, but why I should trust you is beyond me." She shook her head. Ironic, she thought. Not too long ago she had been saying she couldn't trust this dog's owner, and now she was telling his dog she didn't trust it. Well, she would find out. "Okay, Buster. Let's go." Without another word, Olivia headed down the trail, uneasily looking out for Alex. Buster congenially trotted alongside, keeping pace with her easy stride.

The trail narrowed down a hill causing Olivia's flat-bottomed espadrilles to slip on the loose shale. Buster immediately slowed down and let her catch herself on his back. She stopped and knelt down next to him. "You are a trustworthy pooch, aren't you?" she murmured scratching his ears. "What are you doing here all by yourself, anyway? Is your owner going to pop up all of a sudden? I should send you packing far away from me, but you are good company."

"I see you found my wayward dog again," came a voice from further down the trail.

Olivia shot up, nearly landing on her backside. Buster bounded to the man, happily wagging his tail, his whole rear end swinging in delight. She watched the cheerful tail race down the hill and thought *sure, just when I thought I could trust you, you abandon me.* She sighed. She should have known Alex would not be far away.

Olivia, steadied herself against a small birch sapling and watched Alex in khaki shorts and an old grey t-shirt walk up the path towards her. Wryly, she eyed his hiking boots, thinking they were much more appropriate for the trail than her flimsy espadrilles.

They surveyed each other in silence as dusk threw long shadows from the trees and the evening song of birds rang in the air. Olivia's heart thumped so loudly she was sure Alex could hear it. The steel was gone from his silver eyes and the angular planes of his face had softened in the gloaming.

This had been Alex's evening walk all summer long; the only place where his mind could quiet itself. Though the far side of the park backed up to the Meres mansion, he had found another entrance, miles away from the trail that skirted the mansion. Meeting Olivia unexpectedly was the last thing he wanted to do after that disastrous meeting in her kitchen. Yet, here she was in a rosy summer skirt and simple white top, illogically hiking a trail in rainbow-hued espadrilles. The usual colorful scarf held back the raven curls with the inevitable tendrils escaping around the edges.

Buster, sensing a stop, plunked himself down in the center of the narrow trail and lay his head on his crossed paws.

Alex was the first to break the silence. "It seems Buster knows how to find friends in the woods. I was wondering what was taking him so long to get back to me, and now I see why." Buster's ears twitched as he heard his name, but he remained quietly at their feet, occasionally raising his eyelids to look up at them.

Olivia looked down at Buster and felt a small smile try to escape. "Mmm. I thought I had the woods to myself, but apparently not. He is good company on a walk."

Alex looked down at her shoes. He felt sure this walk had not been planned. "Well, since we're both here, would you mind company for a little while, or would you rather be alone?"

Olivia firmly kept her eyes down on Buster. He turned his face up to hers and presented her with the same wide loopy grin. She returned the smile. What harm would it do to walk a ways with these two? Maybe she could put to rest the confusion she felt towards Alex, once and for all. "I suppose company would be okay for a bit, though I'm not really planning on going very far. As a matter of fact, I've really come further than I had intended. I just needed to get out and get a breath of fresh air."

"Ah…That explains the choice of hiking apparel," Alex grinned. "Well, at this point I think you are closer to my car than to your place. Do you want to keep going this way? I could drive you back to Meres on my way home."

Olivia thought a moment. She could just say good-bye and they could go their separate ways and be done with it…or she could take up his offer. Her last encounter with Alex had not exactly been pleasant. Before she really had a chance to think it through she heard herself respond, "Sure. Heading to your car would be fine."

Where the hell had that come from, she kicked herself?

Alex felt a ridiculous surge of joy course through him. What did he think was going to happen, anyway?

Olivia slowly let go of the sapling and started down the steep trail. Instinctively, she put a hand out to steady herself and Alex caught it. Sensing exciting new action, Buster sprang up and started running circles around the two of them, brushing first against the mountain laurel shrubs on either side of them, then against their legs, all the while yipping with elation. "Alex, Buster is not helping. Could you please calm him down before he knocks us both over!" she yelped sliding down the trail.

"Here, boy," Alex soothed his dog as he let go Olivia's hand and grabbed the collar on his neck and attached a leash. "Why don't you go ahead and set the pace. Buster and I will follow behind."

"Fine. Though I warn you, I'm not going quickly. If you get tired of the pace, just go ahead of me."

Alex thought to himself, the slower the better. "I'm not in a rush. Take your time."

Olivia turned around, gained her footing, and continued down the trail listening to the rhythmic breathing and footsteps behind her. Her thoughts were in turmoil. Why was it that anytime she saw Alex away from business, he appeared to be a decent guy? How could he compartmentalize his life so easily? The path leveled off and widened. Alex and Buster now flanked Olivia as her stride lengthened. Furtively, she glanced over. Alex caught her look and smiled.

"Who would have thought a month ago that we would be able to walk side by side like this? You were pretty clear about how you felt about me the last time we met."

Olivia felt her cheeks flame, as she fought to remain cool. She had only spoken the truth. Fortunately, she, with a lot of help, had been able to succeed despite him, yet not every small business crushed by a huge firm survived. "I am trying to separate who you are as a man from what you, as a business person, did to me. It's not easy. Though right now, these woods and Buster make it easier."

"Olivia, business is not always pretty. Sometimes you have to make decisions to survive that are complicated; decisions that move competition out of the way and allow you to grow. Just as you have people working for you and depending on you, so do I. Hundreds, as a matter of fact."

Olivia remained silent. Would she end up making similar decisions? Would she be able to do what Alex had done? Was that the only way to maintain and grow a business?

Alex looked over to her serious face as they continued down the trail. Gently he added, "After meeting you, I realized I would have loved to have had you join the business. Yes, we believed buying those buildings at a discount was necessary, and yes, your business did not appear to pose a big threat. But, you need to understand, once I met you, I really did not want to hurt you. At the time, you gave me no other option."

Olivia stopped walking. "No, I suppose I didn't. But you did not come in looking to see what we were doing. You came in with the idea of taking over the buildings for your own business. Remember? Your first offer was for me to come and work for you as an employee. It wasn't until I was settled at Meres that you talked partnership."

Now it was Alex's turn to remain silent. He had to admit she was right. He had wanted the control. The plan was for his business to take over. After meeting Olivia, he had expected her to join as an addition to *his* business as an employee, not as a partner. "You're right," he confessed. "I wanted control and didn't think anyone could run a business better than I could. I admit it took me a while to get around my own pig-headedness to see you for what you really are...a gifted entrepreneur and chef. Can we call a truce and begin again?"

Olivia looked into the serious dusky eyes that seemed to be asking for forgiveness. How dare he think small business owners were idiots. Where did he come from? Was his business handed to him fully formed on a silver platter? Irritation, anger, and desire fought inside her as she attempted to stay cool and not allow herself to be swept away by the beseeching eyes.

"Perhaps. But understand...we really are still in competition. What new issues are going to crop up as my enterprise grows and we bump into each other again? Why should we begin again?"

"You're right, issues could come up again, but you're helping me appreciate that maybe business does not need to be so cutthroat." He hesitated, then said in a quiet voice, "Because maybe you can teach me something about business."

"Me? Teach you? I don't think so."

He turned towards her, with Buster dancing between the two of them. "Yes. You."

Olivia knelt down to scratch Buster's ears and hide her confusion. Could she trust this man who had the ability to make her heart pound? Were her emotions overriding her common sense? "Buster, help," she whispered. He licked her face companionably.

Standing back up, she faced Alex. "Okay. Truce. Though I'm not sure what that means."

Alex smiled and put his hand out. "It's official. We have a truce. And we'll just have to find out what that means."

She looked at his outstretched hand and met it with hers. Slowly they shook hands, their eyes never leaving each other. Alex felt his self-control disappear. Roughly, he pulled Olivia towards him, cupping his hands through her curls, pressing his lips hungrily against hers.

Shocked, Olivia pulled back for an instant, then felt the resistance melt away as she instinctively responded to the fierce onslaught of Alex's lips. She burned with the intensity, her arms now twined around his bent neck. Buster, excited by the new action, decided to join the couple by jumping up onto the both of them, one frying pan paw on each one's shoulder.

Startled and gasping for breath, Alex and Olivia broke apart, nearly tumbling to the ground. "Shhhh...down boy," Alex soothed Buster. "It's alright," he said scratching him behind his scruffy ears. Shyly, he glanced over to Olivia who had knelt down to pet Buster's back.

Olivia returned the glance. Gently this time, he bent over and put his lips on hers. Slowly they stood up together. She felt the warm lips caressing hers and the fire intensified. Hungrily, she responded, losing sight of anything other than the man who enveloped her at that moment.

Chapter 29

It was Buster who finally decided it was time to move on. Olivia started, remembering that she had told Dan she would be there at seven. She looked up at Alex, feeling his chest rising and falling against her as he stroked her back gently. "I have to get back. I told Dan I would be over at his place at seven."

Alex started and quickly released Olivia. "Dan?"

Olivia laughed shakily at the expression on his face. "It's not what you think. I'm going over for some business advice. He's very much with Tiffany."

Alex breathed deeply. "I need to see you again. I don't know what we started here, but I would like to find out. Do you have any time this week to go out to dinner with me and talk about this?"

Olivia hesitated. "I'll be in the city until Thursday. I'll be back Thursday evening. We could check with each other then, to see what we're up for."

"Thursday sounds very far away right now," he murmured taking her back in his arms. "I suppose I can wait."

"I need to go before I'm late."

"Can't you give Dan a call and cancel?"

Olivia considered this for a moment. Why not? Because she wanted to talk over her idea and needed Dan's advice. Or did she? Could she talk to Alex about this? A jolt of panic coursed through her veins. What had she been thinking of… kissing Alex like this? He still was her competitor!

Abruptly, she jerked away from him and said, "No. I need to go see him…and I don't cancel on friends."

"Ouch!"

"I'm sorry. It just occurred to me that we are still enemies."

Alex looked at her sadly. "We should get back. We're not far from the car. I'll drive you home."

They drove silently the short distance. As she opened the car door to step out, Alex reached over and grabbed her hand. "I'll call you Thursday."

With a tight smile Olivia replied, "Okay. We'll talk," and pulled her hand away.

Alex freed her hand. Released, Olivia felt bereft, the fire still coursing through her veins. She gave a small wave and went in to change without looking back.

Dan smiled as Olivia walked into his back yard. She looked beautiful, her cheeks rosy as though she had been out in the garden all day. Tiffany shyly walked over from the grill. "Hi Olivia, it's really nice to see you, though I must say it scares me to have you eating my cooking," she said glancing over at Dan.

Dan walked over to stand behind Tiffany and put his arms around her waist. "You have nothing to worry about. Your cooking ranks with the best of the best," he said, squeezing her tightly to him.

Smiling at the two of them, Olivia handed Tiffany the bottle of chilled Vouvray she was carrying and said, "I am sure it will be scrumptious. Thank you for letting me barge in on you at the last minute. I'm so used to talking everything over with Dan. He's pretty much the only person I trust to give me good advice."

"Well, dinner is almost ready. Why don't we eat first, then I can let you two talk business. Would that be okay?"

Olivia looked at this sweet young woman so calmly resting in Dan's arms. No jealousy marred the clarity of her gaze as she spoke to Olivia. Dan had chosen well and she hoped they would be happy together for a long, long time. "That sounds perfect. I'm starved!"

An hour later, the three sat comfortably around the outdoor fireplace on Dan's stone patio sipping Calvados, while digesting the delicious dinner of grilled tuna and asparagus. The cheery blaze was doing a good job of keeping the mosquitoes at bay. "That was delicious, Tiffany. If ever you want to moonlight from the firm, come over to my place!" Olivia grinned.

Tiffany laughed and looked at Dan. "I don't know, the firm is a pretty nice place these days." The looks they exchanged spoke eloquently of their feelings for each other. Olivia felt like an outsider looking in on something very private. She shivered in the warm evening air, remembering the lips on her own just a few hours ago.

Dan finally looked over to Olivia and said, "So, what advice do you need?"

Olivia sighed and thought back to the discontent she had felt in the office earlier that day. Her unexpected meeting with Alex layered her thoughts with confusion. Wryly, she thought that the advice she really needed now was about Alex and getting her head examined. She struggled to clear her mind and focus on the issue. The issue was not having enough time to create. She needed help, yet if she was honest with herself, she was afraid to give away the control she held on the business; the control that had led them to financial success.

"Dan, when I was working today I realized that, even though everything is .going more than amazingly well, I have so much paper work that I can't do the things I love to do like creating new recipes. So…I was thinking about getting a business manager to take over on the business end of things. The problem is that I don't really feel comfortable handing the reins over to just anybody…if at all. I guess I need to figure out if this is the right solution, and if it is, where do I find that special person I can trust?"

"Hallelujah! It's about time you realized how hard you are working. I completely agree with you; you do need a business manager. And, I think with the revenue stream coming in now, you can well afford it. As a matter of fact, you may end up being more profitable if you can concentrate on doing what you do best. And you're right; the big problem will be finding the right person to manage the business. Don't be afraid to let go a little. You're not going anywhere; you'll be able to tell right away if something isn't right. Micromanaging is what gets a lot of growing business owners into trouble, from what I can tell from my clients."

Maybe Dan was right and she did need to let go. A glimmer of excitement shimmered through her. Olivia looked at him and smiled. "Okay, oh wise one. So, where do I start looking for this wonder person? Do you know anyone, or have a suggestion of where I could start looking?"

For a brief insane moment, Dan considered taking the position on himself. Olivia's business almost felt like his baby, too. But looking over at Tiffany brought home how much he enjoyed his own career and the life he was creating. After a few minutes of quiet contemplation, he responded, "There's a head hunting firm in New York that does business with us. They specialize in high-end corporate management. They may be pricey, but it might be worth it. Have you thought about how much this position is worth to you?"

"If you're talking about how much salary I can afford to pay, I haven't. This is the very first time I've thought about this. I guess I better crunch a few numbers before talking to any headhunters."

The elation Olivia had felt deflated a bit with the reality of what it might take to find the right person and how much it might cost to bring him or her on board. Nothing was ever simple, she thought wryly.

"You're looking for a very special person, but that person may make all the difference. It might be worth more than you think. I know you may not like this suggestion, but what about talking to Alex Dumaurier about this? He's in the business and may know someone."

Olivia blushed just hearing the name. Her espadrilles became suddenly very interesting and she found it hard to pull her eyes away.

Dan misunderstood her obvious discomfort and said, "I get it. I'm an idiot for thinking of him after everything he's done to you."

Olivia looked up quickly. "No, that's actually not it." Did she want to divulge what had taken place just a couple of hours ago? Right now? No…this was not the time. She herself had not had time to process what happened. "I think I would prefer to speak with a head hunter first. If you could give me the name of the company you deal with, that would be great."

"Sure. I'll text it to you from work tomorrow."

Tiffany walked over with the bottle of wine. "Could I refill your glass?" she asked.

"No, thank you, Tiffany. You've been very patient listening to all this. It's late and we all have a busy day tomorrow. Thank you, Dan. As always, you've helped me think clearly." Olivia gave them both a hug and headed through the star-lit night to her car sitting at the front of the house. Dan and

Tiffany strolled with her, arms entwined around each other's waists. The honeysuckle's sweet scent perfumed the air. Except for her tumultuous thoughts, everything was in perfect order.

Chapter 30

Alex tossed in his bed, finding no comfort in any position. His desire for Olivia was driving him crazy. This was more than a fleeting feeling. Olivia had haunted him from the moment he had laid eyes on her at the Christmas party. This evening, her words, her lips, her scent drove him to the edge of some unknown precipice. There was no question; she was the one he had not known he needed in order to be complete...until now. Somehow, he would have to show her that he was trustworthy, on her side, a partner...in every meaning of the word.

Chapter 31

Just as promised, Dan texted the name of the headhunting firm to Olivia early the next morning. It did not take long for the woman on the other end of the phone to understand what Olivia needed. The problem was going to be finding that special person. Olivia hung up wondering whether she really wanted that person to be found. Letting go to a stranger was not going to be easy.

The next few days flew by in a whirlwind of meetings and tapings for the show. It was only when she woke up in her hotel room at two in the morning did she think about the Thursday dinner. She could not reconcile her emotional and physical reaction to Alex with all the upheaval he had caused in her life. It made no sense. By the time she was sitting on the train headed home on Thursday afternoon, she was exhausted, with little desire to have an emotional encounter over dinner.

Harry greeted her with a hug when she entered the kitchen at the mansion. "We missed you, girl! Welcome home, superstar! You're just in time to meet Edward. He stopped in to see you, and luckily you're here now." Turning around he said, "We've been chatting and he has some divine plans for the Austin wedding." Olivia glanced over to the corner conference table where Gilberta was sitting with a strikingly handsome man sporting a light brown checked Italian cashmere suit with a bright red tie. He rose as she came over to join them.

"Edward Maddox, Claire's wedding planner," he said as he shook her hand. "I have to be honest. I was quite upset when you lost the lease to your store. These kinds of histrionics have no place in planning a wedding. I actually told Claire to find someone else, but she reassured me you were the best and that you could do this. After seeing your facility and meeting your team, I feel somewhat better, but there is a lot to do in a very short time."

"We will not let Claire and her daughter down. This wedding is even more important to us now than ever before. Harry, Gilberta, and the rest of the crew can top anything you will find in Manhattan. This wedding is our focus from now until June."

"That is nice to hear, but I also know you spend half your time in New York taping a show. Do you feel sure you can devote as much time as Claire needs on the event? I still have time to go to someone else. Be honest because my reputation depends on this."

Olivia looked directly into Edward's pale eyes. "We have moved mountains in the last few months to be ready for this event. As you can see the kitchen is ready. The staff is ready. I give you my word that I am ready. If you are ready, we can do a tasting of menu items next Friday. Are you ready?"

Edward glanced over to Harry and Gilberta, then looked back at Olivia. He examined her face, then seemed to come to a decision. "Next Friday at 11:30am. I'll be here with Claire. Her daughter is still in France and will not be home until the following week. I'm assuming all will go well at the tasting, but if it doesn't, be prepared to have Claire go elsewhere."

"She will be very happy, rest assured. See you next Friday, then."

Edward thanked Harry and Gilberta and took his leave. Harry let out a sigh of relief. "Yikes! That was a little harsh. He didn't act like that when we were talking about colors and styles."

"Honestly, I can't believe Claire is still using us. After what she saw us go through, I wouldn't blame her for going to a stable established organization. It's a good thing we've been working on those menus."

"Olivia, how are you going to do everything?" asked Gilberta. "Edward was right. You do have the show. Marta can maintain the website and we can run the cooking school, but that leaves us very thin."

"Hopefully we'll hire a good business manager to run that side. We can use the recipes from the wedding for the show. The show will tape two days a week. The rest of the time will be focused on the wedding. If we have to hire staff, we will."

"Oh! That reminds me. The woman from that headhunting agency called and said she had a couple of resumes for you to look at," reported Harry.

"Great. Maybe we'll have someone soon to help out." Olivia looked at Gilberta and Harry. I think we are on the edge of the big time. Are you guys up for all it will take?"

"Absolutely!" assured Gilberta.

"Are you serious? This is a trip! We are going to rock this!" responded Harry.

Olivia grinned, her exhaustion gone. Just then her cell phone chimed. She glanced down and saw Alex's number. She hesitated, then pressed 'Ignore'. "Nothing important," she said. "It's late. I need to get some sleep. Let's talk tomorrow and see where we are with the wedding and plan out the timeline."

With quick hugs, Harry and Gilberta gathered their things and left, leaving Olivia sitting in the serene space of the kitchen. She had no room in her life for complicated emotions. This was business and that was something she understood.

Chapter 32

Alex looked at his phone as it went to voicemail. Was Olivia somewhere where she received no service, or was she deliberately putting him off? He decided not to leave a message. She would see that he had called. The ball was now in her court. He had work to do and chasing after someone, no matter how he yearned for her, was not part of it. He sighed and scratched Buster behind the ears. Buster cheerfully gave him a lick and curled up at his feet, watching him as he opened his computer and went back to it.

The following morning Olivia reviewed the resumes the agency had emailed her. They both were impressive, but one held her attention more than the other. A young woman, fresh out of Harvard business school, was looking for an independently held small business to begin her career on the ground floor. Compensation was not so much an immediate issue, as future growth and possible profit sharing. A few phone calls later and Kaiya Kennedy was scheduled for an interview the following Monday. Next was to meet with Harry and Gilberta to begin planning their strategy for the execution of the Austin wedding.

They came in to find Olivia placing a basket of warm croissants and a pot of hot coffee on the expansive conference table. She greeted them with a smile, nearly bouncing on her toes, hardly able to contain all the ideas bubbling to come out. It felt so good to be working hard on what looked like a very bright future. Her notebook already contained two pages of notes written while waiting for her two friends. The taping of the show, though exhausting, had gone very well and now she was going to have a lot of fun planning the most exquisite wedding. She had no room for other thoughts.

Four hours later, Gilberta came back from the printer holding the sketched out menu for the hors d'oeuvres, first course, entrée, and desserts. Cocktails would be accompanied by tiny little pastries, some made with roasted corn and fresh thyme, others to be filled miniature cornucopias of crisp potato filled with crème fraiche and caviar. Colorful cascades of blanched crudité with be stationed in antique wooden bread bowls, with thick dips of all kinds circling like jewels on a crown. Nothing would be drippy, everything would be just big enough for one tiny bite of flavor. Lilliputian lobster rolls and doll-sized glass flutes filled with chilled sorrel soup would grace displays made of 200-year-old barn wood. Fairy lights would lend an air of enchantment. Olivia knew this was a good menu from top to bottom. The first course of slivers of lightly salted grilled cod over a dollop of vegetable risotto with a truffle emulsion would burst with crisp and creamy flavors, yet be light enough not to overwhelm the main course. The entrée choices of pan roasted squab or crusted red snapper would satisfy even the most discerning French diner. And finally, the desserts. The cake would crown the evening, but that would come later, after hours of dancing. To end the meal, a light bite of sweetness would tease the palate. Mango parfait would glisten in tiny hazelnut dacquoise cups, with shards of chocolate adorning the plates. It was perfect. Harry and Olivia sighed as Gilberta handed them the copies of the menu. Claire Austin would be delighted, they were sure.

"I'm starving!" Harry stated standing up and stretching. "What's for lunch?"

Companionably, the three seared salmon, put together a salad, and sat at the table to eat lunch all the while discussing the next cooking video and sales of the new cookbook. It was when they were sipping coffee that the kitchen phone rang. Harry answered, listened, then paled. The police department wanted to speak with Harry and Olivia about a suspect. Could they come over to the mansion to talk to them in 15 minutes? Olivia nodded her head slowly and Harry put the phone down.

"Harry, I know this is upsetting to you, but maybe this will put an end to the whole thing once and for all," Olivia soothed him as he came back to the table looking tense.

"I hope so, but if it really is Tommy who broke the vent and the window, and now the smoke bomb, I'll never forgive myself for getting involved with him," he said miserably.

Gilberta stood up and put her arms around him. "You're the world's nicest person. A little naïve and gullible, but absolutely the nicest," she smiled.

"Just because some schmuck became obsessed with you, doesn't mean any of this is your fault."

"I agree," said Olivia coming around the table and putting her arms around the waist of both of her friends. "This is a good thing. Hopefully the mystery is solved and we can continue forward." Flashes of accusing Alex of the vandalism flashed through her mind. Alex. And Harry thought he was a mess with his relationships. She sighed.

The knock on the door made them all turn around to face the same trim policewoman who had been in the store in December, accompanied by a portly young man dressed in plain clothes. They gathered around the table to look at photographs of a car, an apartment building, and a close-up of a man coming out of the apartment.

"After speaking with you the other day, we followed up on your friend..." began the policewoman.

"He's NOT my friend!" Harry protested.

"Sorry about that. We followed up on Thomas Stewart and found that he owned a red Toyota, just as you said. We found it parked outside this apartment building. We were able to get prints off the door which matched the prints on the rock at the store and the prints from the break-in here this winter. It seems pretty clear this man is involved with at least two of the incidences you have reported," she stated nodding towards Olivia.

Looking over at Harry, the detective added, "We are going to need you to make a statement that this is the same car you saw in front here, the other day, as well as at the street light by the store back in January. Do you think you can do that?"

"Yes," he answered firmly, looking determined. Then tremulously, he added, "Is he going to be locked up? I want to do this, but I'm a little nervous about what he could do to me."

"We are holding him for questioning, but we may not be able to keep him behind bars. We can issue a restraining order against him if he gets released."

"Why did I have to go out with this creep!" Harry wailed.

Once again, Olivia put her arm around his waist. "You had no idea. Who knows how attraction works," she sighed thinking of Alex's number on her phone. "We'll get through this, just like everything else."

Harry left with the officers to make his statement while Olivia and Gilberta cleaned up lunch and began planning for the tasting the following Friday.

As Olivia worked, she kept thinking about Harry's lament. Why was she so attracted to Alex? He had been a creep, too, though admittedly in a different way. And yet just the thought of him made her blood rush. She could not get involved with him. Not now. Life was too busy and full of exciting possibilities, that made her blood rush without Alex. At some point she would have to let him know she was not going to see him again. For the moment, she would put him out of her mind and concentrate on the production schedule for next Friday.

On Monday morning, a young woman with flaming red curls that were trying successfully to burst out of a demure headband, knocked hesitantly at the kitchen door. Harry, who was sitting at the conference table placing the rental order for the tasting, looked up from his computer. His eyes widened as they traveled from the striped green leggings, which led to a burnt orange skirt topped by a grass green tunic. Intelligent blue eyes peered through glasses that looked like they were borrowed from Harry Potter.

"May I come in? I'm here for a nine o'clock appointment with, I believe, a Ms. Caron."

Guiltily, Harry jumped up, aware that he had been staring for far too long. He wondered if his mouth had been gaped open the entire time. "You must be Kaiya," he blurted as he shook her hand.

"I try to be," she returned with a broad smile.

Harry was in heaven. If this person knew how to handle a business, she'd fit right in. He led her over to the conference table. "Make yourself comfortable while I go get Olivia," he said as he nearly danced a jig to the back storeroom to find her.

"Your appointment is here," Harry trilled back to Olivia, who was deep in the reaches of the storeroom shelves.

She came out with a quizzical look on her face, her arms laden with containers of olive oil and vinegar. She looked at Harry who was practically dancing while grinning like the Cheshire cat. "Harry? Is there anything I should know about this person?"

"Oh, you'll see. Come and meet Kaiya." He took the containers out of her arms and led the way back to the conference table.

Immediately, Olivia understood Harry's delight. But could this young woman take care of the financial side of a business? Kaiya stood up as Olivia approached and held out her hand. Well, she was polite and did not appear shy. Olivia shook her hand warmly. "Good morning. Would you like some coffee or tea while we chat?"

"No, thank you. It would probably go right through me, I'm so nervous."

Olivia smiled and looked into the eyes of this earnest young woman. Behind her glasses, the eyes were clear, beaming with intelligence and honesty. A nervous furrow ceased her brow. "Have a seat. Let's talk about what we need and what you can do for us. Harry anchors the business here, so he'll be interviewing you as well," she said nodding towards Harry.

Kaiya took a seat and handed Olivia her resume. It did not take long for Olivia to realize that Kaiya was sharp as a tack. Glancing over to Harry, she could tell that he was just as impressed. She caught his eye, and with a small nod, made a decision. "I think I can speak for the both of us and say we would love to have you work with us."

Kaiya let out a whoop of delight. Olivia smiled. "Does that mean you'll join us?"

"Yes! When can I start?"

"When can you start?"

"Today?"

Olivia laughed. "Why don't we say tomorrow? We have a tasting to prepare and need to get organized. Tomorrow, you can trail us and get the lay of the land. After the tasting, we'll have more time to actually show you what needs to happen. Sound good?"

"Sounds perfect," Kaiya beamed.

The kitchen felt nearly bereft of color after Kaiya left. Olivia looked over at Harry, who still appeared somewhat stunned. "I hope we did the right thing. I think we did. I probably should have called her references before hiring her, but I just have this really good feeling about her."

"If she is everything she appears to be, she'll be wonderful," agreed Harry. "Why don't I call the references this afternoon, just to be on the safe side."

Olivia looked at this newly cautious person. "Seems to me you have learned a lesson from this whole Tommy business!"

Harry nodded his head. "Yeah...not every pretty face can be trusted," he said wryly, "though this time I think it will work out."

The week disappeared as the team worked on all the preparations for the tasting. Kaiya had arrived, dressed in bright orange sneakers topped with green overalls over a white T-shirt. Her hair had been tamed under a blue bandana. Olivia thought about all the ways this young woman could have dressed for her first day at work as the business manager. High heels, grey suits...none of which would have been appropriate. She realized that they had never discussed how she should dress, and she was grateful that Kaiya astutely had recognized the need for sensible shoes and contained hair. It bode well for the future.

While Kaiya installed herself in Olivia's office, Olivia, Gilberta, Lena, and the rest of the staff stirred sauces, chopped, and prepped for the big day. Olivia was confident Claire would love the menu, but she was still anxious that everything be perfect. There was no time or room to think about Alex. Not even the sight of his number on her phone distracted her from her work.

Edward called Thursday to confirm for the following day and Kaiya expertly handled the call. Edward had set the phone down impressed by the cool, polite efficiency of the young woman responding to his questions.

Kaiya came down to the kitchen to let Olivia know Edward had called. She looked around and saw that the conference table now looked like an elegant dining table. A shimmery pale grey tablecloth was topped by a lacy cream overlay. Platinum-rimmed cream china sat at each place while neatly folded pale grey hem-stitched napkins with cream colored menus tucked inside lay on the top plate. Porcelain place cards sat above each place setting. Thin-stemmed wine glasses stood next to sturdier stemmed water goblets. In the center on the table lay a low floral display of blush and cream roses tightly meshed together with sprigs of ivy. To her untrained eyes, the table looked like it came from a fairy tale, it was so beautiful.

The kitchen smelled heavenly, though most everything had been tucked away for tomorrow. "I've never seen anything so beautiful!" she exclaimed, coming over to Olivia and Lena.

"Thanks," said Lena.

"Hopefully, Claire will think the same thing tomorrow," added Olivia.

"Oh. That's why I came down. Edward just called to confirm tomorrow."

"Great. We're all set. I do have one thing to ask you. Tomorrow we need to dress formally. The waiters will be dressed in their black shirts and dark blue ties with long black bistro aprons. Gilberta and her staff will be in chef coats. I'm going to wear a formal dress. Do you have anything you could wear that is a little formal?"

Kaiya looked dubious. "You mean like what I wore Monday for the interview?"

Harry came over. "Maybe I could meet you at your place and help you put an outfit together. What do you think?"

"Well, if it's that important." She looked over at Olivia. "Am I going to be seen? Can't I just stay in the office and work?"

"I think it's important for you to be involved in all parts of the business to understand everything that happens. Seeing this type of tasting will show you what we go through to conduct business and why we charge what we charge. You also may see things with fresh eyes that we don't see."

"As long as you don't ask me to cook or serve anything!"

"No worries. We won't," laughed Olivia.

Chapter 33

Alex sat in his office, a frown darkening his face. The meeting with the catering director had not been pleasant. Apparently every social event for the next year had already booked with Sweet Sage. What was left were the corporate lunches and meetings. Where the magical name of European Gourmet opened the door to every socialite's home in all his other locations, here it seemed to slam them shut. It appeared that rather than putting a competitor out of business, he had invigorated it. Not only that, but it had been a week since he returned from Chicago and Olivia had not yet returned his phone call. He could feel the ball of frustration building inside his chest. This eastern flagship of a store was not off to the start he had anticipated due to the only person he wanted to be with more than anyone else…and she appeared to have slipped away again, out of his reach. A little known sense of powerlessness swept through him. Where had he gone wrong? And here he was questioning himself again. European Gourmet would not be where it was today if he had second-guessed himself along the way. Damn it! He may not be able to have Olivia, but he could continue to make a success of his business. Abruptly, he stood up. His catering director would simply have to find a way to break into the market. If not, he would find the person who could. And he would call Nicole and ask her out to dinner. She had been a perfectly pleasant date and would most likely welcome a call from him.

Friday morning, Kaiya entered the Sweet Sage kitchen with a nervous smile. She was dressed in a simple red skirt topped by a black knit shirt dotted with tiny watermelon slices. Her legs were sheathed in black stockings and her hair was gathered in a loose chignon. Olivia, dressed in a pale grey sheath of a dress, smiled at her across the room. "You look professional and cheery. That's a perfect outfit for today."

"Well, thank goodness for Harry. I wouldn't have thought of so much black. I kind of like it, too. I like my colors, but I guess sometimes it's nice to change. Do you need help with anything, or should I go up and work on the books?"

"Harry is going to be here any minute and Gilberta has been here since early this morning with Lena, so I think we're good. Thanks for offering. We're going to have a quick meeting as soon as Harry arrives, so why don't you work on your things until he gets here, then you can join us."

When Claire Austin walked through the front door of the Meres mansion, she had not expected to find such an elegant, bright and modern kitchen. It was obvious that this was not a business struggling to get by. The savory scent of thyme drifted towards her from little round crisps cooling on a rack. Another rolling rack stood in the corner laden with Lilliputian golden pastries. Serving trays of all types stood ready for service, with little white hemstitch cocktail napkins stacked neatly nearby. She was surprised by her sense of relief. Maybe she had been worrying, after all. She looked around and spotted the carefully set table in what appeared to be a conference area. Just as she started over to get a closer look, Olivia came through a door in the back of the kitchen, Gilberta in tow.

"Claire! My apologies! I didn't hear you come in. Welcome to the new and improved Sweet Sage! Do you remember my sous-chef Gilberta? Gilberta will be preparing the menu for us today."

"Hello, Gilberta. Of course I remember seeing you in the back of the store and at my parties. This is quite an impressive kitchen! It must be a joy to work in compared to the old one at the store."

Gilberta nodded in agreement. "We always made do with what we had, but I must admit, it is much easier to work here. Speaking of work, I need to get back to that kitchen or we won't have a tasting!" she said laughing and headed back to the kitchen where Lena was already preparing hors d'oeuvres.

Claire turned to Olivia. "Olivia, I have been following your career and I am not at all surprised that you are doing so well, but my dear, do you have the time necessary for this wedding with all you are doing? This really cannot be something you do on the side. How will you manage the television show and everything else you are doing while giving the wedding the attention it needs?"

"Claire, you have to believe me when I tell you your daughter's wedding is the single most important part of our business right now. Until every guest has left and everything is cleaned up, your family's wedding is our number one priority. Yes, I'm busy, but I have a phenomenal staff to keep all the balls in the air. Sweet Sage is not just about me. Yes, I create and direct, but it takes a team of talented, hard-working people to do it well."

"Wow! I feel even better than I did a minute ago!" said Harry, as he walked into the room.

"Claire, do you remember Harry? He was the front manager at the store. He now is the catering designer and front staff developer. He will also be the floor captain at your daughter's wedding."

"Hello, Harry. I do remember you at the store. If you can run the waiters as well as you ran the store, we're in good hands," she smiled.

A knock on the kitchen door alerted them to Edward's arrival. The suit he wore looked just as expensive as the last one, but this time it was pale grey with a deep blue silk tie. Olivia caught Harry staring and gave him a quick bump to bring him back. Kaiya came down the stairs just as they were heading over to the table. Now it was Harry's turn to be amused by the look on Edward's face as he caught sight of the mass of red hair and Harry Potter glasses over the watermelon speckled top.

"This is Kaiya, our new business manager," said Olivia as she went over to lead a shy Kaiya to the table with her. "She just graduated from Harvard Business School and will be taking over on all those jobs that kept me out of the kitchen. I asked her here today as part of our team. Everyone has to understand every part of this business, or it doesn't work."

Claire looked at Kaiya, then thoughtfully at Olivia. "I believe I have made the right decision in staying with you through all your changes."

Edward, eye brows raised, looked dubious. Stepping closer to the set table, he had to admit that he had not seen finer in New York. The porcelain name cards were a nice touch and the low floral arrangement of pale pink and white roses with moss was elegant and practical. Guests would be able to speak to each other across the table without having to peer around one of those horrid gargantuan displays. But could the food and the service match the design? He had his doubts. And if it did today, would they be able to perform on the day of the wedding? Really. If only Claire would listen to him and let his tried and true connections do the wedding. Even at this late date, they would guarantee an excellent result. Plus, he knew how they worked, never mind the kickback they always rewarded him with after the event. This could be a nightmare. Just look at that girl in her atrocious watermelon top. It looked like bugs had landed on her grandmother's sweater.

Edward had to admit, at the end of two hours, that the food was excellent and the service staff had performed well. They, at least, looked professional in their black shirts and long bistro aprons. He knew Claire was delighted by the tasting, but he still wished he was working with staff he had worked with before. It was easy to run a two hour tasting. A three-hundred-person wedding was a whole other ballgame. He sighed irritably.

Claire set down her coffee cup and looked over at Edward. "Edward, do you have any comments? Everything I've tasted was delicious and the service was lovely." She looked over to Harry. "The delivery of the food to the table was impressive. I had not thought that we could have each person at the table receive their food at the exact same time, but the way your staff worked was superb."

Harry blushed. "We practice that a lot. I hate waiting for my food when waiters have to go back and forth. This system takes a little more staff, but everyone at the table gets served at the exact same time. No waiting for the last person to get served while your food gets cold. Each waiter always comes out of the kitchen holding only one plate in each hand, and all the waiters for one table come out at once, single file. They place the plates in front of each guest at precisely the same time. Just like today. It never fails. Good service done well is like a ballet."

"Yes, but can you do this when you have three hundred people to serve?" interjected Edward skeptically.

"This is how we serve at all our big events. You are welcome to call some of our clients to ask them how we did," he responded defensively.

"Edward," Claire stepped in, "as I have said before, I have had Olivia and her staff cater many of my cocktail parties. I would not have chosen Sweet

Sage to cater Ella's wedding if I didn't think they could do it." Rising, she turned to Olivia. "Please continue the planning with Edward. I'm sorry to say I have an important committee meeting to go to in an hour, so I need to get going. Thank you for an excellent tasting. Just those few changes we talked about, otherwise the menu is perfect. I'll be in touch." She turned to Edward. "My secretary sent over the guest list to your office as you requested, along with Ella's requests on how she would like the wedding to flow. I'll leave it to you and Claire to sort out the logistics."

"Thank you. My staff sent over a copy. I have it right here."

"Please give me a call on Monday to give me the update."

"Certainly."

"Good. I look forward to hearing from you." With a good bye nod to Olivia, she strode out the door.

Olivia contemplated Edward. "We may not be New York, but we are world class. I am going to assume you are as good as you say you are because Claire hired you to be her wedding coordinator. I would appreciate it if you gave us the same courtesy. If you do not agree with something, let's talk about it like adults."

"My reputation rides on the last event I produce. I can't afford even one tiny slip-up. Claire may trust you, but I've never worked with your team before, and to be honest, this is the first I've heard of

Sweet Sage. Maybe you are as good as you say you are, but until I see it for myself, I'm going to be on the lookout for disaster."

"You won't find one. Now, what if Harry, Kaiya and I go over the guest list and wedding flow with you to make sure there won't be any of those disasters? We can't finalize a seating plan until all the RSVPs are in, but we can begin to sketch it out."

Gilberta signaled to Lena to have the wait staff clear the conference table. In just a few minutes, Olivia, Harry, Kaiya and Edward were poring over the list that included each guest's relationship to the bride or the bride's family. Claire had wisely added notes about special concerns she had regarding certain guests. It was up to Edward to create the perfect seating plan. Kaiya didn't utter a peep the whole time, but absorbed all the information. For someone who had never dreamed of getting married, let alone in a fairy tale wedding such as this, envisioning the reception from the string quartet ushering in guests, to the final goodbye and the drive off in the limousine, was a shock akin to watching an alien landing in the front seat of her Toyota. The tasting alone had been a remarkable experience, but the discussion of the tents, flowers, quartets, bands, and specialty toilets for the guests made her feel like she was on another planet. The notebook she had brought along just in case was filled with notes and questions to talk to Olivia about later on.

It was five o'clock before they knew it. Gilberta, Lena and the staff had already left when

Olivia sat back and stretched in her chair. "I think this is a good beginning. We have it sketched out pretty well. The seating plan isn't perfect, but until you speak with Claire to clear up those few issues, there's really nothing more we can do right now. Why don't we call it a day?"

Edward grudgingly had to admit that these no-nonsense people had been sensible and creative. "That would be fine. I'll call you Monday afternoon, after I have had a chance to speak with Claire. I, of course, will need to be at the meeting with the tent and lighting people. Let me know when they are available to make sure the time is good for me. Can your team do that?"

"Absolutely," Kaiya jumped in.

Olivia looked at her in mild surprise, then smiled. "Kaiya will call you when she has the details."

Edward rose and held out his hand stiffly. "Well, I have to admit today did go well. Let us hope that things continue to go just as smoothly. I'll be in touch." He gathered his briefcase and let himself out the door without any further comment.

"Whew! Glad that's over! A real sweetheart, isn't he?" exclaimed Harry. "And look at you, all set to work," he added grinning at Kaiya.

Kaiya blushed. "I don't know what came over me. Wait, yes, I do. Edward was being insufferable. You guys just put on an incredible show and he's treating you like lackeys. I couldn't stand it, so I jumped in. At least I can organize a meeting for you, even if I am brand new."

"I think you are going to make a great addition to our team," Olivia said. "Come on. Let's go to the office and I'll give you those numbers."

"And if you're not too tired, I have some questions about today," responded Kaiya.

Olivia studied this wild-haired young woman for a moment. Maybe hiring a business manager was going to be very good thing. She owed Dan a thank you.

Chapter 34

At home that night, Olivia snuggled in her window seat with a glass of wine, just thinking over the day. Kaiya had been a wonderful surprise. Edward had been a pill. Harry and the team had rocked! The wedding was going to be a joy to execute. She felt certain the guests were going to truly enjoy the menu and the ambience was divine. She could see the rose spotlights dancing among the flowers and gauzy fabrics twirled around the tent posts. The birch branches holding fairy lights over every table would lend an air of magic. She loved creating and felt sure that with the addition of Kaiya, she would have more time to play with recipes and designs.

Dan. Now was the time to call Dan to thank him for showing her the way and providing the connection to the agency who found her. She reached for her phone to press his number and caught a fleeting glimpse of Alex's number, still sitting there on her call list. Maybe the wine had loosened her guard. She so wanted someone to hold her, care for her, listen to all the incredible things that were happening all around her…make love to her. The memory of the steamy embrace in the woods sent shivers through her. She could still feel the strong arms embracing her, the hands weaving through her hair; lips hungrily pressing against hers. She could feel the muscles in his arms; the feel of his chest pressing against her. Heat flooded her body. It wasn't

Dan she wanted right now, it was Alex. Her finger hovered over the number. Then pressed.

"Olivia! I was just thinking about you," Dan's cheery voice came ringing through the phone. "Today was the big day, wasn't it? How did it go?"

Taking a deep breath, Olivia began to tell him about the crazy week, the tasting, and best of all, her new business manager. By the time she got off the phone, her emotions were back in control. Dan and Tiffany had listened breathlessly together on speakerphone to every detail of the tasting. And Dan laughed loud and long when he heard about Kaiya.

She had dear friends. She did not need the trouble of an Alex. One day she would find the right person, and now was not that day. She had a busy weekend ahead getting ready for next week's shows. She headed for bed

Chapter 35

Claire's daughter Ella had arrived in the states with a portfolio full of wedding cake ideas from France. Olivia had gone to Claire's home with cake samples for her to taste and photos of some of her past work. Ella had been dazzled by the photos and impressed with the quality of the cake samples. Together, they had come up with a design based on one of Olivia's photos. It would be simple and elegant. As a nod to her French family-to-be, Ella had requested small pyramids of pastel macarons of all colors and flavors to be placed on the table around the cake, along with a few golden pyramids of airy cream puffs held together with gossamer spun sugar. The cake cutting ceremony would crown the evening.

The kitchen hummed all week with wedding preparations, recipe testing, and class preparations. Gilberta and her crew came in early every morning to produce the day's items, leaving the kitchen ready and clear in the afternoons for Olivia's baking and show preparations. Olivia placed the last cream puff shell in the container for the freezer with satisfaction. They were all ready to be filled and glazed right before the wedding in two weeks and they were perfect. When she returned to the kitchen from the walk-in freezer, she found Harry sitting on a stool, his shoulders slumped and his chin in his hand.

"Harry! What's wrong?"

"The police just called. They released Tommy on bail. He has a restraining order and can't come anywhere near me, my house, or where I work, but I'm worried that won't keep him away."

Olivia sighed. With Tommy in jail unable to raise bail, they had felt a sense of security. Harry was right. There was no telling what Tommy would do now, especially since Harry was the reason he had been caught and put behind bars. She couldn't imagine he would be any smarter or nicer now.

"Oh, Harry…"

"You know, I'm actually not so much worried about me, as I am about you and the business. Just look at what he did over the holidays to the store. Everyone knows the wedding of the century is happening in two weeks. I wouldn't put it past him to try something then."

Olivia mulled this over. He was right. They did have police ordered for the wedding to prevent gate-crashers and to make sure there were no problems, but she had not thought about something like this. "I'll have Kaiya call the department and let them know our concerns. I think we should have a bigger police presence there than we have already contracted for. I'll have her ask them to patrol us often for the next couple of weeks, too. Even if it's just a smoke bomb, I don't want to take any chances."

"I'm so sorry, Olivia."

"Hey! I've said it before…this is not your fault. Chin up, old man! We have work to do."

Harry lifted his chin out of his hand and straightened his shoulders. "Yes, Captain."

"That's better. Let me go up and see if Kaiya has had any more phone calls from dear Edward and fill her in on the Tommy situation. Are you all set with the staff for the wedding?"

"Almost. I need a few more waiters and I'm still trying to make sure everyone has the proper uniform. We're going to have a rehearsal next Thursday and I'm going to have everyone bring in their uniforms to leave with me. I'm going to send them all to the cleaners to make sure they are clean and pressed and waiting here for them. I'm not taking any chances."

"Great. What time is the rehearsal? I'd like to have a staff meeting with them when you are finished rehearsing. I should be back from the city around 4pm. Would that work?"

"That sounds about right. They all arrive here at 1:30, so that should be about when we are done."

"Perfect."

Olivia left to find Kaiya, while Harry headed to his office to make phone calls.

She found that Edward, like clockwork, had called again. This time he was fretting about the behavior of the staff behind the scenes during the wedding. He was demanding absolute silence in the prep tents. And cooks were not to bang pots or make noise of any kind. Olivia sighed. She knew Michael chose his staff carefully and trained them well. No one had been disruptive in the past, and no one was going to be disruptive in the future. And no one was going to bang pots! By now she knew that a quick phone call to smooth his feathers would go a long way, so with another sigh, she picked up the phone and called.

    Alex was fully aware that the biggest social event of the year was just around the corner. Even his uncle Leo, though not invited to the wedding himself, was somewhat involved. An old acquaintance of his, Phillipe Legrand and his wife Paulette, were flying in from France a few days ahead of the wedding. They would be staying at Leo's house and Alex had been invited to join them for dinner the day after they arrived. He had arranged for European Gourmet to cater the intimate dinner. Now the only question was whether to invite Nicole to accompany him or not. She was perfectly nice and was not demanding more from their relationship, if that's what you would call it, than what he was willing to give…which was almost nothing, he had to admit. Nicole was pleasant and she relieved that physical longing…somewhat, but he did not want to involve her in his life more than she already was. He decided not to bring her along to the dinner.

    Reviewing the week's numbers, he was relieved to see that foot traffic in the store had increased and sales of ready-to-eat fare and groceries had gone up. The coffee bar was also beginning to show activity, particularly in the morning. They were far below the standards in his other locations, but they were moving in the right direction. It was the bookings for social catering that remained abysmal. No doubt about it, it was time for a new catering director. European Gourmet had strong directors in other sites. The thought of moving someone to this store crossed his mind. But the problem here was not so much that he didn't have a good director, it was that the town trusted a catering company that had been here before him and was still here now, stronger than ever. How could he bring the town to trust his company, when admittedly, a charming, creative, and competent alternative was still there? The town did not seem to need two such businesses. A thought flickered through his mind and, in horror, he pushed it out almost as quickly as it had entered. Sabotaging Sweet Sage's biggest event would seriously damage their reputation. His conversation with Olivia about business echoed in his mind. He could justify taking over a business, but he could not justify falsely damaging a business reputation. What kind of monster had he become that that kind of thought even crossed his mind? And there was Olivia again. Directly in his path. Ferociously intelligent, creative, hard-working, driven. Womanly, soft, desirable. Time had not softened the heat that flowed through his veins whenever he thought of her. He could still smell the faint lavender on her skin when he had held her. He had felt her response and knew he had not imagined it. They had a connection, whether she wanted to admit it or not. Her catering business was the perfect match for his store; she was the perfect match for him. He got up and walked over to the window that looked down on the town's main street. The maple across from the fire department shone pale green with the fresh new leaves of spring. He knew what he had to do…but he would have to be patient and bide his time until after the wedding.

  Dinner with the Legrands was more fruitful than Alex had imagined it would be. The distinguished couple were close friends of the groom's parents who managed a large cheese exporting business. Though Alex already had his purveyors lined up, the possibilities of expanding the cheese departments in all his stores with a French partner was intriguing. Phillippe had mentioned that his friend was looking for a more direct outlet for his products. The volume that European Gourmet could generate was exactly what he had been looking for. He would set up a meeting with the five of them after the wedding. The meal had continued amicably, with the catering staff doing an admirable job with the courses and service. Phillipe and Paulette Legrand had been quite complimentary. Alex had purposefully chosen a classical American menu including freshly shucked clam chowder and rosemary cornbread. A superb apple pie with a sharp cheddar crowned the meal. Alex did not think Sweet Sage could have done a better job. There had been an awkward moment when Paulette had asked who was catering the wedding and why it was not European Gourmet. Alex tried to deflect the question by simply saying Claire had booked the event with a caterer who had been in the area for quite some time long before European Gourmet had come to town.

Leo, with a few too many drinks under his belt, let out a guffaw. "Yes. And the joke's on Alex! He thought he was taking her out by buying her building and kicking her out, but she came roaring back! And she's pretty cute to boot!"

Phillipe and Paulette looked at Alex with interest, sensing there was more to the story.

Alex glared at his uncle. "It's true, I did buy her building. But she received a generous settlement, which she used to set up a commercial kitchen and continued to cater. I have to say, she is very good."

"Well, it will be very interesting to see how she does with the wedding this weekend. Will you be attending?" asked Paulette in French. Until that point, the conversation had taken place in perfect, if heavily accented English. Alex wondered if Paulette was tiring, or if she was simply aware of the staff and trying to be more circumspect.

"No. I look forward to hearing all about it when we meet," Alex responded easily in French, wondering if this woman was so perceptive that she had already picked up the undercurrent of his feelings for Olivia.

Turning the conversation back to cheese and importing regulations, Alex was able to steer away from Olivia and back to his uncle, who happily pontificated on the legalities of importing raw milk cheeses. The evening ended with Alex in an upbeat mood, feeling better than he had in quite a while. He knew what he had to do. He smiled in anticipation.

Chapter 36

The wedding day finally arrived with overcast skies. Olivia quickly looked at the weather forecast as she rose from bed. No rain - just overcast. Okay, that worked. They would not have to put the tent walls down, which meant that the dining area and dance floor would not be a steamy mess.

By 6am, Olivia was in the kitchen checking the to-do lists and reviewing the timeline for the reception. As she started on her second cup of coffee, Harry appeared.

"So I guess I was not the only one who couldn't sleep!" he teased her affectionately.

"I know everything is in complete order, but for some reason, this wedding feels different. I feel like more is on the line this time than has been in the past. And that is completely foolish, because every wedding is important!"

"True. But you have to admit it's a minor miracle that we are here today. Just think of what was happening six months ago."

"It has been a wild ride." She took a sip of coffee and looked thoughtfully at Harry. "We are so ready for today. Ella and Claire are going to be thrilled." Who was she trying to reassure here?

"I know, Sweetie," Harry sighed. "It's just my damned pre-party jitters. And I've got to tell you, that pill of an Edward is not making it any better. I swear, if he calls to go over one more time how the bride and groom are going to be served the entrée,

I'm going to cut off his precious Italian silk tie at the neck!"

"Now that would be a sight!" she laughed. "Go grab a cup of a coffee and we'll go over everything to make sure we haven't missed anything."

Across town, a red Toyota slowly drove past the gates of the Austin estate. The driver's face was hidden by a low-slung baseball cap. When a police car turned into the short street, the car sped up, quickly took a left turn into the nearest street, and disappeared.

"Hey! Did you see that?" the young officer asked his partner.

"Yeah. You didn't happen to get a license number, by any chance?" he responded over squealing tires as he turned the patrol car around and sped back to where they had just come from.

"Nope. He turned too quickly."

"Okay. Let's see if we can catch them coming out this end."

There was no sign of the Toyota anywhere. "Damn it! I don't have a good feeling about this. That car sure as hell looked a lot like the one the captain warned us about."

"I agree. What if we drive by that guy who is out on bail, make sure he's home," suggested the younger man.

"Great minds think alike," responded his partner already on his way there.

They drove up to the apartment and found the red Toyota sitting primly in front.

"Damn!"

The older officer parked behind the car and stepped out. He went over and placed his hand on the hood of the car. You could fry an egg on it. He returned to the patrol car and radioed in to the captain. Unless there was an exterior camera on the gate, they could not prove that this was the same car they had just seen, but it damn well probably was. They needed to run a patrol by the Austin estate all day. The last thing they needed was to have the town matriarch's daughter's wedding ruined by a crazy man out on bail.

Alex woke up from his dream feeling like he needed to accomplish something important…but he couldn't remember what it was that he needed to do. Lying in bed, he ran down the list of what he knew he had to do that day, the most important being to chauffer his uncle's acquaintances from France to the wedding that evening, as he had offered to do. The wedding. The wedding that Olivia…Sweet Sage…was catering. This was the biggest event of the season. Maybe this was what had him in such a state. What was it? That Sweet Sage had the catering locked up, or that Olivia would be there? That he needed Olivia…for more than he wanted to admit. Olivia…her scent, her lips…everything about her drove him to the edge of sanity. He sighed and got up. Immediately, Buster loped over to get his morning scratch behind the ears. "You love me;

don't you Buddy?" he murmured into Buster's ears. Abruptly he stood up. He had a plan to deal with Olivia. It was all worked out with his uncle, of all people. All he could do was his best, then let the chips fall as they may. He stood up and headed down to start his day.

    Harry and Olivia had finished the review of the day's schedule when Kaiya, dressed in a fuchsia pink top with black leggings, walked in the door.

    "Hey, Pipsqueak, what are you doing here so early?" teased Harry.

    "Are you kidding? This is the most exciting day of my life! I've never been to a wedding, never mind this kind of wedding. Plus, I want to help. What can I do?"

    "You can relax and help check in staff when they arrive later. Meanwhile, I think we're okay. Have a cup of coffee…or maybe not," Harry grinned.

    Gilberta, Lena, and the rest of the back-of-house crew started arriving. Vans began to be loaded and the first wave was sent out to the Austin estate to begin preparations. The florist arrived shortly after to drop off flowers for the wedding cake table and the hors d'oeuvre trays. Tents had been set up since Thursday to guarantee dry, firm ground, and the rentals had all been checked in the day before. By noon, glimmers of sunshine began to peak through the clouds. Olivia smiled. Two phone calls from Edward, regular as clockwork, the sun was shining…life was good. She went home to change into her wedding outfit.

Chapter 37

That afternoon, Olivia, dressed in an off-white and pale silver linen business suit, was under the dining tent supervising the first wave of waiters who were busy with the initial set-up of the tables. The dance floor was set and Edward was thankfully busy dogging the saintly patient florist, as he put the last touches on the tent pole wrappings, giving him unsolicited advice. Harry would arrive shortly with the second wave of waiters and the bartenders to complete the table settings and set up the bars. Olivia had brought the wedding cake over in separate tiers. It was sitting happily in one of the refrigerated trucks parked and left running next to the garage behind the cook tent. She would assemble the cake just as the guests arrived for the ceremony, which was to be held on the hillside beyond the tent overlooking the bay. Sunset was at eight, and guests were scheduled to arrive at six. There would be no danger of a hot sun melting down the cake. Edward had made sure that there was a spotlight strategically placed to highlight the cake. In fact, all the lighting, from the gauzy chandeliers over each table to the fairy lights on the poles and the rainbow lights on the dance floor, was spectacular. Once the sun had set, the tent would become magical. Grudgingly, she had to admit that Edward's eye for drama was excellent.

By 5:45, Edward had long disappeared to supervise the first photo shoot with the family.

Olivia, Kaiya and Harry walked up the gentle slope to where the ceremony would begin shortly. The weather, though never completely cloud free, was balmy and calm. Secretly, Olivia was glad the sun was not out in full force to overheat guests and wilt flowers. Harry brought her over to the reception area to review the passing trays and the bars. Glasses of all types shimmered in the evening light. Fairy lights hung in the trees on the edge of the gathering area. The bay over the hill provided a majestic background, with the few remaining clouds accented by the golden pink of the setting sun. Kaiya sighed.

"It is beautiful, isn't it?" Olivia said. "I never get tired of this moment, when all the tiny bits and pieces all of a sudden meld together to create magic."

Harry nodded. "The calm before the storm."

Olivia glanced up at him. "Nervous anymore?"

"Nope. We're all good. Just look at the staff," he said proudly waving his arm across the expanse to the small army of waiters standing at their posts, ready to welcome guests.

Olivia noticed the first few guests making their way to the bank of chairs for the ceremony. "There's my cue to go finish the cake. Kaiya, want to come and help?"

The two took off for the cook tent behind the garage, leaving Harry in his tux to supervise the seating of the guests.

As Olivia crossed the driveway to the cook tent, she noticed a familiar black BMW coming to a stop in front of the garage doors. Her heart leapt as she recognized the driver. Their eyes drew to each other as though held by a powerful magnet. Kaiya placed her hand on Olivia's arm. "Hey. Are you alright?"

Flustered, Olivia tore her eyes away and looked at Kaiya blankly. He wasn't on the guest list! What was Alex doing here?

"Olivia?" Kaiya repeated as she peered through the dusk into the car to see who it was that had given her such a start.

"It's nothing. I just didn't realize someone I knew was going to be here," she replied, abruptly moving on towards the cook tent.

They turned the corner behind the garage to where the refrigerated trucks were parked. Odd. Olivia had parked the cake truck last in line by the other two. It was not there now. Olivia led Kaiya into the tent where another small army, this time of cooks, busily worked on long rows of steel tables under bright lights. Gilberta and Lena circulated and directed amongst them. The sight was orderly, humming with synchronized efficiency. Kaiya stood still, a look of sheer amazement on her face. Olivia walked over to where Gilberta was showing a cook how to design the passing trays for a particular hors d'oeuvre. "It looks like you have everything beautifully under control here," she smiled.

Gilberta looked up, a look of concentration on her face. "We've got a good crew and the set-up is working well. Everything is on schedule."

"Great. I'll just grab my cake things and get out of your way. I see the cake truck is not out there. Thanks for sending it out to the tent."

Gilberta looked confused. "I didn't send the truck out. Maybe Lena did. Hey, Lena! Did you put the cake truck out by the tent?"

Lena looked up from her dip bowls. "No, sorry. Do you want me to drive it over?"

Olivia and Gilberta looked at each other, then simultaneously ran out to the trucks, Kaiya following close behind. There should have been three trucks. Just as Olivia had noted before, the third truck on the far end was missing.

With her heart beating like a drum, Olivia nearly sprinted back to the dinner tent, looking for any sight of the truck along the way. It was nowhere to be seen. This couldn't be happening! Trying not to panic, Olivia scanned the estate grounds and almost as though in an alternate reality, she noticed Alex escorting an elderly woman to her chair in the ceremony area. Suddenly, she knew what she had to do. She turned to Kaiya. "Kaiya, can you please bring me one of the officers? I think there are four here. Gilberta, go back to the kitchen and carry on. The wedding needs to go off seamlessly. Worst case scenario, we'll only have the dessert table cakes, but I'm going to do everything I can to find the wedding cake. Please don't say anything to anybody, especially not to Edward. I don't want to start a panic. Even without a cake, this will be a fantastic wedding."

Kaiya took off in a pink blur. "We'll be fine," Gilberta responded calmly, but grimly as she headed back to the cook tent.

Olivia looked through the dusk now full of twinkling lights to where she had seen Alex with the couple. He was walking away now, heading towards the driveway. Quickly, she headed towards him, knowing she had no right to ask him for help, yet somehow feeling in her gut that this was the right thing to do. He saw her coming, and with a look of surprise, turned to greet her with a small smile playing on his lips.

"Olivia, everything looks…"

"Alex," she interrupted hurriedly, "I know I have no right to ask this of you, but I need help."

This was not the greeting he had expected, but then, he didn't know what he had expected. All he knew is that his plan to avoid Olivia at all costs in order not to distract her on this important day was happily out the window. "I'm happy to help, if I can. What's going on?"

Olivia looked into the eyes that she had seen burn darkly with heated passion, yet could flash with the cold of steel. Now, they were filled with smoky concern. Gratefully, she realized that her hunch to ask him for help had been right and she took a deep breath. "It appears that someone has stolen the refrigerated truck with the wedding cake inside. I have no idea how it could have happened, but now we don't have a wedding cake. Do you think there are any cakes at your store, or do you know of any wedding cake that we could go pick up at this late hour? I would be happy to remake whatever cake we borrowed tomorrow."

Alex tried to digest what he had just heard. It was not what he had been expecting, to say the least. "Are you saying someone drove off with your truck that held the wedding cake."

"I'm not one hundred percent sure, but right now I don't have any other explanation for why it's missing. I drove it over here myself and left it running to keep the cake refrigerated. It would have been pretty easy for someone to drive away with it."

Alex remembered that as he had been about to enter the driveway, he had had to wait a moment as a Sweet Sage truck had exited. It looked perfectly normal, so he had not thought anything about it. "Do you remember when we saw each other by the garage?"

Olivia nodded, blushing.

"I had to wait a few moments before entering the driveway as the officers let one of your trucks out. It seemed perfectly normal at the time, but that must have been it."

"Did you happen to see who was driving?"

"Not really. I was busy talking to the Legrands. Though, I think it was a fellow wearing a red baseball cap."

Olivia paled. Tommy? Again?

Alex looked at her in concern. "Do you think you know who it was?"

"Maybe," she whispered. "Let me talk to the police. Meanwhile, I need a cake or a few smaller cakes for the ceremony. I have a few macarons tiers and cream puffs, but I need cake for the ceremony. If we don't find this one in time, I'll need something and I don't have extra cakes lying around in the walk-in."

"I don't know what I can do to help, but let me call the store to see what they have. My pastry chef might still be there, and we might be able to put something together. Let me call."

Alex took out his phone to begin making calls as a policewoman walked up to Olivia. Olivia finished giving her the rundown of what she knew as Alex got off the phone. The officer turned to Alex. "Could you tell me what you saw?"

"Honestly, it wasn't much, but when I was arriving, I had to wait a moment for a Sweet Sage truck to finish exiting before I could enter the driveway. That might have been the truck with the cake."

"It probably was," Olivia interjected. "We only have three trucks, and only one is missing, so it had to be it."

"Did you happen to see the driver?" the officer asked Alex.

"Not well. I wasn't really paying attention to that. I vaguely remember a man wearing a red baseball cap, though."

Olivia turned to the policewoman. "I don't know if you are aware, but a man named Thomas

Stewart was arrested for damaging my business. He is currently out on bail awaiting trial. I know this is a long shot, but he used to wear a red baseball cap."

"Thanks. He can't be far. Let me call this in," responded the policewoman. "By the way, does the truck have GPS?"

"Yes."

"Do you know the license number, off hand?"

"No. I'm sorry."

"No problem. We can get it. I'll call if we find anything," she said walking away.

Alex turned to Olivia, who was still pale, but now seemed calm. "I spoke with my chef. He is going to call the pastry chef in to put something together. He looked in the walk-in and it looks like there are some cakes baked that she could use. It will probably take a couple of hours before we can get anything here."

"Thank you," Olivia responded quietly. Alex had no reason to help her. She had pushed him away hard.

Alex would do anything to take away the shadows on her face. "Don't thank me yet. Go back to what you were doing. I'm going to go and make sure the pastry chef knows what we need. I'll be back in a couple of hours, if not sooner."

Olivia watched as Alex left, then looked one last time at the empty table before heading over to the ceremony area. Whatever happened, she would make it work. The guests had a dessert for the meal.

One way or another, there would be some kind of cake available for a ceremony. No matter what happened, it would be fine, she repeated to herself.

By now, most of the guests had arrived and the string quartet was quietly playing in the background. Nothing more was going to mar this wedding. Harry smiled at her as she walked over to him. He looked poised and well under control, with every lock of his blond hair neatly slicked back. He did not need to know about the latest problem.

"It's a perfect evening. It's so peaceful here," he said looking around with satisfaction at the staff working efficiently on the gently rolling slope overlooking the bay, tent spires in the background.

"Mmm...," Olivia smiled wanly.

Guests were quietly chatting at their seats as the long-aproned waiters passed around champagne flutes of sparkling water holding one jewel-like raspberry. The sky now held a brushstroke of pink as the sun met the water over the bay. Looking over to the dinner tent, Olivia's heart sank. Edward stood glowering by the empty cake table where the wedding cake should have been displayed. Two minutes later, he was walking up the slope to where she stood by an old oak tree, his face a dark storm cloud.

"Didn't we agree to put the cake out as the guests were arriving?" he snapped.

"Yes."

Edward stared at her. "So…where is it?"

"It's coming."

"It's coming!?! Where is it? I thought it was here?"

"Shhhhh. You're raising your voice. It will be. Relax."

"Relax!?!" he hissed. "How can I relax when the main centerpiece is not here and you won't tell me where it is?"

"We had a slight change in plans. It will be here shortly," Olivia said, praying she was right. "Isn't the wedding going smoothly so far? Look how gorgeous everything looks. I hope you are videotaping this for your portfolio."

Edward ignored the last comment and simply huffed.

"You'll have to excuse me. Gilberta asked me to come by the kitchen when I had a chance. I'll be back at the ceremony in a few minutes. Shouldn't you be with the bride?"

Edward just glared at her.

Olivia managed to escape and, as she walked to the kitchen tent, looked surreptitiously at her phone hoping there was a call from the police. It was discouragingly blank.

As Alex headed across town to his store, Olivia dominated his thoughts. As much as her business affected his, he really did not want her to fail this evening. But he had to be honest with himself. This was an opportunity to help her out and, just maybe, it would crack open the door to her heart. Perhaps his plan would not be necessary after all.

Darkness was setting in. Sitting at the light waiting to take a right onto Main St., he noticed a white box truck just ahead. The light turned green and the truck quickly took a left away from the center of town. Even through the dark, he could see the Sweet Sage logo clearly marked on the side. Instantly, Alex called 911 and followed the truck to the left. The truck sped down the busy street, nearly hitting a car exiting a McDonald's. Alex sped up, doing his best not to get into an accident as he tried to explain to the operator on the line where they were heading. The truck took an abrupt right onto a small street. Alex did not see a street sign, and unfortunately was not well enough versed with the area to clearly explain to the 911 operator where they were. They sped under a highway overpass, heading to an area of old warehouses. The truck's speed increased dramatically, bouncing over pot holes and swerving around curves. Alex felt sure the driver knew he was being followed. Even if he was able to stop the truck and get the cake back, he doubted it would be in any shape to be displayed. Alex managed to give the operator the license plate number of the truck as it now swerved behind a warehouse. Following, he saw that the road abruptly ended at a dense stand of trees. The truck stopped and a man wearing a red baseball cap flung open the back gate of the truck and faced the black BMW as it pulled up behind. Alex noticed a glint reflected from his headlights in the man's hand. He could hear the 911 operator tell him to stay on the line; that the police had a fix on his location and were on the way.

Alex slowly opened the door to his car. Standing behind the door, he calmly said, "You don't want any more trouble than you already have. Put the knife down and give me the keys to the truck. At this point you'll only be charged with theft and not assault."

"You think you're so smart, fancy pants! What's it to you? Hunh? You another one of those Harry lovers protecting him from me? I told him I'd get him, didn't I? That bitch he works for never liked me. I know she turned him against me. Now she'll be sorry. You want your precious cake back? Make it worth my while," the man sneered as he threatened to plunge the knife through the satiny white frosting of a wedding cake tier anchored to a wooden shelf next to him.

"I don't carry much cash on me, if that's what you're talking about," responded Alex trying to think of how he could keep this man from destroying the cake before the police arrived.

"Sure you don't. Guess I'll just have to have a slice of cake instead," he said plunging the knife through the frosting then scooping up a chunk of cake with the blade, all the while looking at Alex.

Alex cringed. "Okay. Let me see what I have in my wallet."

"Don't try anything funny. If something comes out of your pocket besides a wallet, this knife will be in you instead of the cake."

"Understood," Alex replied quietly raising both hands in the air, then obviously reaching one hand into his back pocket to take out his wallet. Wallet in hand, he opened it and took out several bills.

"Thought you said you didn't have much cash."

"It's not much." Alex counted. "I only have $120.00 here. You can have it all if you don't damage the cake any further and give me the keys."

The man thought it over. "Okay. You step out from behind your pretty boy shield and put it on the hood of your car. You come any closer and I'll do this all over you," he said slashing the cake one more time.

Alex cringed again watching Olivia's work get wrecked. "I said no more damage or you don't get this!"

"Well then, put it on the car, hotshot."

Alex came out from behind the door and very deliberately walked to the front of his car.

"What 'er you waiting for? Put the money down and get back to where you were before. You think I'm stupid?"

"Toss the knife away from you and I'll leave the money on the hood."

The man seemed to contemplate this, then smiled. "Sure. Why not." With little notice, the knife flew past Alex's ear.

Alex gritted his teeth and placed the money on the hood, then backed slowly towards his open car door, all the while watching this crazy man and wishing the police would hurry up and get there. It felt like hours since he had called.

"Get behind the door and don't try anything funny!"

Alex obeyed. The man jumped down from the truck and while one hand reached over for the money, the other grabbed another knife hidden in his belt. Instead of dropping the keys on the hood, he grabbed the money and started to run towards the woods. Without thinking, Alex leapt out from behind the car door and chased him. Just as they reached the pines, Alex lunged forward and managed to tackle the man's legs. With his face contorted with hate, the man lunged at Alex with his knife, striking him in the shoulder. Alex swore, but held on to the writhing body. Out of the corner of his eye, he saw two police officers run up and pull out their guns.

"Both of you, lie on the ground, face down."

Alex froze, then carefully slid off the boots he had been lying on and lay face down breathing heavily. His shoulder throbbed.

With both guns trained on the man with the red cap, one officer asked Alex to identify himself.

"Alex Dumaurier. I called 911 and followed this guy who was driving the stolen Sweet Sage truck. May I sit up?"

"Sorry about that Mr. Dumaurier. Sure. You can get up." Turning to the man in the red cap, he said, "You stay down." He walked over to where the knife lay and kicked it away. "Your arm is bleeding. How badly are you hurt?"

Alex winced as he rose. "I'll live, but I probably should get a bandage on it. By the way, you'll find another knife somewhere over by my car. He was well supplied."

The police handcuffed the man, yanked him to his feet, and led him to the squad car. Alex walked over to the truck and looked into the back to assess how much damage had been done to the cake. One tier looked awful, but the other four tiers looked nearly as good as when Olivia had finished frosting them. A minor miracle, as far as he was concerned.

He walked over to the police car. "That cake inside the truck is meant to be at the Austin wedding right now. Any chance we can get it there before going to the station?"

Just then, two more squad cars pulled into the parking lot.

"Sure. Let me arrange it with these guys." He went over to where the other officers were standing with the cuffed prisoner.

Alex looked impatiently at his watch. It felt like hours had gone by, but to his astonishment, it had been only a little more than thirty minutes since he had left the wedding. He quickly took his phone and called his store to let them know they know longer needed the emergency cakes and then he called Olivia.

The wedding ceremony was just about to end when Olivia felt her phone vibrate. She took it out and saw the name written there. Alex. It had only been half an hour. Walking quickly down the slope, she answered it on the fifth ring, just as it was going to voicemail.

"Olivia! I have your cake. There's some damage to one tier, but most of it is fine. We'll be there in about fifteen minutes."

Olivia didn't know whether to laugh or cry with joy. "Thank you, thank you, thank you," she whispered.

"I'll be escorted by police, but we'll try to be discrete. See you soon." And he hung up.

The officer had retrieved the truck keys from Tommy and taken a bandage out of his First Aid kit. He walked back to Alex, just as Alex got off the phone. "We're all set. These officers will take the suspect back to the station. I'll drive the truck and we'll have my partner follow. Let's go, but first let's put something on that arm." He wrapped the bandage around Alex's arm, then closed up the back of the truck. Alex climbed into the truck's passenger seat gratefully, fatigue washing over him.

Fifteen minutes later, the truck and one squad car quietly drove through the gates of the Austin estate. Olivia and Kaiya were there to greet them. Immediately, Olivia spotted the bandage on Alex's arm and the dirt that adorned both knees and the entire front of his once pristine jacket. She looked at him in alarm. "We'll talk later," he said. "Right now come and look at the cake."

Olivia looked at the stabbed tier. Anger swelled through her, then she clicked into business mode. "Kaiya, please go to the kitchen tent and bring back two carts back with someone to help. Let's get these tiers over to the wedding cake table. I'll go gather my equipment and meet you there." Looking over to Alex, she said, "I have to deal with this right now. You need to go take care of yourself. I'll call you later, if that's okay?"

"Call me, no matter how late it is," Alex said, brushing back the lock of hair that would not be tamed.

"Alex, I don't know how to thank you. I'm..."

"Go. We'll talk. Right now you have a wedding to deal with." He gave her a quick kiss on the cheek, then headed back to the squad car for a lift to the emergency department.

Olivia stood there for a moment, her hand on her cheek. Then she snapped back to the wedding, her focus squarely on the cake. In the twilight, she could see guests off in the distance mingling under the twinkling lights as waiters glided through passing hors d'oeuvres. She would be able to work on the cake with no interruption...or so she thought.

"What the hell is going on? I just came by the dinner tent and saw the wedding cake tiers. It's a disaster!"

Olivia turned around to find Edward glaring at her.

"Nothing that a little magic can't fix. Go away, so I can call it in. Shouldn't you be taking care of the photo shoot or something?" responded Olivia, heading to the cook tent to retrieve her buttercream and cake decorating tools.

"We'll talk about this when we have our debrief tomorrow," he snapped at her. "Right now I need to know that that cake will be up and ready before the bride comes down that hill."

Olivia looked at him. Holding her tongue, she managed to say simply, "I'll do my job. You go do yours."

Edward glared at her, then stomped off to the back porch where the photo shoot was under full swing.

Olivia breathed a sigh of relief and went in to get her things. Gilberta looked up from filling an hors d'oeuvre tray. "Kaiya told me you got the cake back, but that it didn't look great. Anything I can do to help?"

"No. Thank you. I think it's mostly the bottom tier that looks bad. Let me go work on it. I'll call if I need you. How's it going back here?"

"Great. Looks like we'll have plenty of everything and all the stoves are working well. We're prepped for the dinner, so everything should be right on schedule."

"I'll check in with you as the reception ends. Assume everything is on the same schedule as planned. I'll let you know if anything changes."

"Aye, aye, Captain," Gilberta grinned, sending off the waiter with the filled tray.

Olivia returned a lop-sided smile, then left to do damage control on the cake. Despite the rough ride, the four top tiers were in good shape. The new shelving with the fitted wooden boxes had saved them from total destruction. The bottom tier was a different story. A large gash and a missing chunk the size of a fist marred one whole side of the cake. Since the cake design was geometric and smooth, Olivia could not use flowers to hide the damage and she did not have enough buttercream to fill in the gaping emptiness. The cake would have only four tiers. That's all there was to it. Luckily the design would still look finished and complete, even with only four tiers. It was the height that would be missed. Olivia looked at the wooden cake box that held the tier. She called Lena and asked her to send someone over with an extra set of table linens and a large silver tray. She got to work filling her pastry bag with softened buttercream and took out her tools. By the time she had flipped the empty cake box onto the center of the cake table, a young cook was there with the linens and tray. Olivia neatly covered the box with a linen and overlay, then set the silver tray on top. Carefully, she lifted each tier out of their box and set one on top of each other. Taking her pastry bag, she slowly piped pearly beads where each tier met the one below. Half an hour later, the cake stood majestically in its place of honor. Olivia stood back and surveyed her work. It would do. No one would guess this had not been the plan all along.

Kaiya gave her a quick hug and took the pastry bag out of her hand. "Let me clean up and put all this back in the kitchen tent. Go up to the reception and say hi to Harry. He's been looking for you."

Olivia texted Edward before heading up the hill to Harry. Maybe he would relax now that the centerpiece was there.

Harry stood off to the side of the reception, watching as the glasses were bussed and hors d'oeuvres were being passed. Olivia came over to him. "Harry, it looks wonderful."

"It does, doesn't it?"

The bride and groom beamed as they greeted their guests. Olivia spotted Claire in her beaded ecru silk and taupe gown. Claire caught her eye and made her way over to where Olivia and Harry stood next to a cascade of colorful vegetables surrounded by baskets of artisan breads and vibrant dips.

"It's just lovely. Just as I had hoped," she said taking Olivia's hands in her own.

"I'm so glad you're happy."

"Well, Ella's in-laws are already suitably impressed…which I must admit is nice," she added. "They can see that France does not have a monopoly on great food and service," she laughed. "I must get back. See you at dinner."

"See you at dinner," Olivia responded. Claire was happy, which meant Ella was happy, and that's all that mattered. Everything, at the moment, was perfect.

Olivia watched the reception hum along, the tent glowing in the background, soft music coming from the quartet. She felt her cheek, the memory of Alex's kiss still there. He had rescued her instead of letting her fail. She knew it would have been to his advantage to have something go badly wrong tonight. And yet, he had risked himself to help. How did all the pieces that made up Alex fit together? Ruthless, logical, determined, passionate, and kind. Where did she fit in with them? Was all fair in business and love?

Her reverie was interrupted by Harry. It was time to move the guests down to dinner. She called Gilberta and told her to fire up dinner, then went to Claire to ask her to lead her guests to the dinner tent. The most technically difficult part of the evening was about to begin.

Olivia, Harry, Gilberta, and Lena took their positions and set the dinner in motion. Olivia timed the service of the courses by alerting Gilberta to the pace of the guests under the tent. Waiters moved in unison, just as practiced. Like a well-oiled machine, the first course was served, the bride's table first; wine was poured, and the toasts began. Edward glided up to where she stood next to the waiter's entrance. "I have to admit, it's going pretty well so far," he said grudgingly. "That's a pretty good fix on the cake."

"I told you I had magic."

"Maybe."

Olivia glanced at him. Edward was no different than Harry, though it seemed to take him longer to get over his jitters and the way he expressed himself was poles apart. It was fear and nerves that made him so unpleasant. By the end of the wedding, he would be a pussy cat.

Olivia excused herself to go back to the cook tent, where Gilberta was just finishing the set up for plating the entrée. The staff was working with military precision. The squab came out of the oven with crispy golden skin and the snapper went in. Hot plates, preplated with the vegetable and garnish, were being held on rolling racks, ready to receive their entrée, while a team stood at the end of the line ready to sauce the plates as they left the kitchen. Gilberta and Olivia nodded to each other, then Olivia left to go back to the tent.

The evening flew by with plates coming back to the bussing tent clean; a good sign. Before Olivia knew it, the cake had been cut, the bride and groom had departed, and only a few guests were left on the floor dancing to the last strains of the music. Gilberta's staff had cleaned up the kitchen and were heading out. Gilberta, Harry, and Olivia met in the kitchen tent. Kaiya came in from loading a truck. They looked at each other silently for a moment.

"Mission accomplished," Gilberta was the first to speak.

"We make a good team," said Olivia, reaching out to them all for a hug.

"Yeah," Harry sighed, tired but content.
Just then Edward entered the tent and paused at the scene before him. Olivia looked up and saw the look on his face. "Edward! Just the person we were missing! We were just saying how all your touches made this wedding so special."
Edward looked skeptical, then pleased, and walked over to the small group. "I know I can be bossy some times," he paused as Harry threw him a look, "but I have to admit you put on a wedding to challenge anything I've seen in Manhattan. I'd even work with you again."
Olivia ignored his last remark and gave him a hug.
They stood quietly for a minute, absorbing everything they had just experienced. Finally, Harry said, "It's not over yet. Some of us must go back to work. Olivia, go home. I can handle the clean-up."
Olivia nodded. "I'll just go say my goodnights to everyone then take off. I'll see you two on Monday. Kaiya, I'll drive you back to the shop."
"I'm going to stay here and help Harry with the clean-up. I'll see you Monday," she replied. "I want to see how everything works from the very beginning to the very end."
Olivia smiled. "Sounds good. Monday it is."
Edward went off to make sure the parents of the groom were all set, while Olivia left to go find the mother-of-the-bride. In the soft night air, she could hear the singer crooning Louis Armstrong's "A

Kiss to Build a Dream On". She felt her cheek again thinking of Alex.

Under the tent, only a few guests remained. She saw Claire dancing on the dance floor, her cheek resting on her husband's shoulder, her eyes closed. Olivia stood quietly on the side of the tent until the music stopped playing. The couple stopped dancing and just stood silently, looking at each other. It was a moment so private, Olivia felt she was intruding just by watching. She turned away and slowly walked over to the wedding party's table to wait for them, wondering if she would ever take part in such a scene, rather than being on the sidelines.

Claire and her husband walked up to her a few moments later, their arms entwined around their waists.

"I just wanted to say goodnight before taking my leave. Harry will make sure everything is shipshape before he leaves with the staff. We'll be back on Monday to make sure the rentals and tents are taken care of."

Mr. Austin took Olivia's hand in his. "This was a spectacular evening. We can't thank you enough."

"I'm so glad you're happy," she responded. "The whole team put their hearts into making this day perfect."

"And it was. Now, go home. You deserve some rest. I'll see you on Monday," Claire said giving her a kiss on the cheek.

Olivia took her leave and walked over to the truck that had held the wedding cake. Like it or not, this was her ride back. She peered into the back of the truck, just to make sure there was no one there. She laughed at herself, yet the drama that taken place there just a few hours ago still raised the hairs on the back of her neck.

She climbed into the driver's seat and headed back home. Tomorrow would be soon enough to bring it back to the mansion.

The light was on in her kitchen, just as she had left it. Fatigue washed over her as she parked the truck in her driveway. The golden glow of her kitchen greeted her as she walked in, but tonight it didn't soothe her the way it normally did. She wanted to wrap her arms around the person she could count on to be there in thirty years; the person on whose shoulder she could rest her head when she was tired…or dancing. Her hand went back to her cheek. Alex had saved her tonight. It was his kiss she thought of. She had to be honest with herself, it was his arms she wanted around her forever. She had said she would call him when the wedding was over, but it was one in the morning. Then she remembered his injured arm. The middle of the night or not, she needed to know if he was alright. She sat down in the window seat, took out her phone and pressed his number. He picked up in one ring.

"Olivia!"

"Alex…how's your arm?"

"It's fine. I was incredibly lucky, The knife did not sever the muscle. A few stitches and some physical therapy, and I'll be good as new. Were you able to use the cake?"

Olivia relaxed and smiled into the phone. "I'm so glad your arm will be okay. And…I want you to know how much I appreciate what you did. I don't think I can bear to hear the whole story right now, but I do want to hear every detail. And, yes, I was able to use the cake, thanks to you. When I asked for your help, I didn't expect you to actually rescue the cake."

"Hm. I didn't expect that either. I hope one of your wedding cakes doesn't get stolen again, because I don't think I'm cut out to be the hero!"

Olivia laughed, then fell silent.

"Go to bed. I'll talk to you tomorrow," Alex said quietly.

"I don't think I can fall asleep, I'm so wound up. It always takes me a while to decompress after a big event, never mind the whole cake story." Olivia looked around her kitchen. She wanted to hear the story of the cake rescue, but most of all, she wanted Alex here with her.

"I must admit, I'm a little wound up myself."

Olivia hesitated a moment, then, "Can you drive?"

"Yes. Why?"

"Would you like to come over for a night cap? I would like to hear the whole story of your adventures."

"Are you sure?"

"I'm sure."

"Yes. I would love it. I can be there is twenty minutes. Does that work?"

"See you then," Olivia responded.

She set the phone down on the window seat and kicked her heels off. Her sheath of a dress still looked good as new despite her active day, but her hair was escaping the pins that had held it neatly in place. She considered changing, but decided not to.

What had she set in motion, she wondered. Tucking a loose strand behind her ear, she kicked her shoes aside and went to look for wine glasses and something to munch. Suddenly, she was ravenous. She opened the refrigerator door and took out cold rosemary chicken, carrot fennel slaw, and her homemade lemon chervil mayonnaise. There was a baguette on the counter. She sliced the chicken onto a plate and opened the bottle of Sancerre. Five minutes later, there was a knock on the door.

You're being ridiculous. Calm down, she scolded herself as she went to open the door. Alex stood there in the glow of the porch light, his arm in a sling, looking at her as though for the first time.

Olivia stood stock still, silently gazing back at the chiseled features accentuated by the shadows. Finally, she dared look up into his eyes…and her knees turned to jelly. "Come in," she whispered, widening the door to let him through.

Alex stepped towards her, gently put his good arm around her shoulder, and pulled her to him. His eyes spoke volumes as he lowered his lips to caress hers. Slowly, without thinking, Olivia put both arms around his neck and immediately became lost in a fierce hunger for this man. Alex felt the flames coursing through his body as he responded. Everything he had longed for, he held in his arms. The identical inferno held them both in its sway.

"Olivia," he finally managed to breathe, "we better slow down or I may not be responsible for my actions."

Olivia stepped back, stunned at the intensity of her feelings. "Maybe we need to talk about this." She closed the door behind him and led him into the kitchen. Alex looked around the warm room, thinking of the time he had been there before. Nothing had changed; it still felt very right. Olivia poured them each a glass of wine, then invited him to sit on the window seat next to her. Olivia leaned against a soft green pillow that was propped against the wall. She tucked her legs under her, adjusting her skirt. Alex settled himself against the opposite wall, at a safe distance.

Both started to speak. With a soft chuckle, Alex nodded to Olivia to begin. "Before we talk about what just happened, I need to know how you came to rescue the cake today."

It did not take Alex long to tell the story. Olivia turned pale as she listened to the account of Tommy's knives. Luckily, he was back in jail, but Alex had come very close to serious harm. She looked at him sitting there in his jeans and button-down shirt with the open collar, calmly explaining the drama. He favored his arm a bit, but otherwise, seemed unruffled by his experience. "And you know the rest. What I want to know is how you were able to fix the cake."

"I technically didn't fix it. I simply did not use the bottom tier and raised the remaining four tiers on a riser to give it the same height. No one has said anything yet. I'll see what Claire has to say on Monday. I'm not sure she noticed." Laughing a little, she remembered the look on Harry's face when he finally saw the cake table after coming down from the reception. "Poor Harry was a little confused. I haven't told him the story yet. I didn't want to upset him during the event. He feels bad enough for everything Tommy did already."

Alex gazed at Olivia as she spoke. He could imagine spending evenings with her just talking about the day's work, then retiring to the bedroom. He slapped down that thought as his body again leapt to respond.

"You must be exhausted and I should get going," he said, putting his wine glass down on the floor, rising from the bench, and walking over to Olivia. "Though this may not be the best time to talk about what just happened, I think we should."

Olivia stood up, skirted around Alex, and walked over to the wooden table to set her glass down. She turned, her back against the table, her hands gripping the edge behind to give herself the balance she needed. "I am tired, but you don't need to leave quite yet. I agree we should talk."

Alex walked over and tucked the stray lock of hair behind her ears. "I have tried getting you out of my system since we met, but I can't. I need you in my life. Is it wishful thinking on my part, or is it possible that you feel something for me, too?" Without waiting for her answer, he gently caressed her lips with his.

His lips were warm and Olivia desperately wanted more, but she backed away and stepped aside. "Yes," she breathed shakily, "but unfortunately there is the little matter of our businesses in the way. You are still my competitor on a couple of fronts."

"Maybe we can work something out."

Olivia thought of all the work she had put into reinventing her business and how well it was going. As much as she needed Alex, she needed her business, too. "Alex, I can't disappear into your corporation, just because I have feelings for you."

"Maybe you don't have to. There must be a way to sort this out. I have to admit my brain is not firing on all cylinders right now, so maybe we should talk about this later. What is important at this moment is that…I need you in my life and don't want to lose you again."

Olivia silently shook her head. She had come home wishing there was someone there to talk to and share her day. Here he was and she was pushing him away.

Alex reached over and softly cupped his hand on the nape of her neck. As his lips came down to meet hers he murmured, "I love you," and kissed her deeply. Olivia wasn't sure she heard the words or imagined them, but right now she didn't care. She released the table and wound her arms around his neck, kissing him until she was nearly breathless. She felt the muscles in his chest pressing against her and inhaled the musky sandalwood scent as he released her lips to nuzzle her ear. Pulling back for a moment, she asked, "Would it hurt your arm to stay the night?"

"No," he whispered huskily.

Olivia took his hand and led him upstairs.

Chapter 38

Olivia studied the sleeping man lying next to her. His face looked almost boyish with his unkempt hair flopped over his forehead and one arm flung over his head. His eyes opened as she looked on. A slow smile spread over his face as he reached over to pull Olivia into his arms. Olivia snuggled close, one hand exploring the body that had given her so much pleasure the night before.

Alex grinned. "You better watch what you're doing, before something happens."

Olivia smiled and continued.

The sun was far up in the sky by the time they were showered and companionably making breakfast in the kitchen. Neither spoke as they fried bacon and toasted slabs of homemade bread. Last night had been like a fairy tale, no worries intruding on the sheer physical pleasure they took in each other. Alex had proven to be a skilled and considerate lover, despite the stitches in his arm. Olivia had forgotten what that felt like; if she had ever known. Her time with Michael had been good, yet different. And it had been so long ago. Now Olivia felt shy, yet contented. It felt so right to be in Alex's arms. She glanced at Alex as he drained the bacon on paper towels with one hand, his other arm back in its sling. He caught her glance and smiled, somewhat looking like the Cheshire cat.

At the table, Olivia buttered Alex's toast for him as he took his first sip of steaming coffee. "Hmmm... a man could get used to this."

"Don't get too comfortable. I expect you to pull your own weight as soon as that arm is mended," Olivia laughed. They ate silently for a few moments.

Olivia sipped her own coffee, looking thoughtful. Reality was beginning to intrude on the fairy tale. "Alex. We need to talk about our businesses."

"We could wait a little while."

"We could, but I don't think we should."

"Olivia, your business is a perfect complement to European Gourmet. We have the physical foot print and you have the catering and media. We could create magic together."

Olivia knew this was true, but she did not want to disappear into the shadow of something that had almost destroyed her. "I think we have very different philosophies about how to run a business. You are willing to expand physically to grow at any cost..."

"That's not completely true," he interrupted.

"Pretty true. Look at what happened to me. Anyway, my way to grow is to look for other opportunities such as the internet, books, classes, that kind of thing. Both grow a business, but I think my way does not destroy people along the way."

"Maybe, but your way does not end up employing as many people as my way. TV shows and books are somewhat solitary activities. Catering employs more staff, but not on a regular basis. But…this is also why I think our businesses would complement each other so well."

"Sweet Sage is like my family. The staff are my friends. How can I join European Gourmet and maintain my friendships and the name to my business? I can't. Imagine if someone was taking you over and you had to give up the name of European Gourmet. Not only that, but European Gourmet is based in Chicago. My catering business is local, based on relationships I've developed over the years. How would that work?"

Alex sat quietly, one hand wrapped around his coffee mug. It was true that European Gourmet headquarters were in Chicago. Eventually, he would have to go back. He could envision Olivia continuing with her TV program and book writing from Chicago, but that would change the nature of her business and her relationships. He thought about the name of his business disappearing. It was an identified brand that was nationwide. It wouldn't be possible. Olivia was right. Unless…

"What if we joined as partners, with east coast stores named Sweet Sage and European Gourmet remaining the name on the western stores? We could move the headquarters to the mansion, so you could stay on the east coast and continue with your TV show. We'd have to travel to Chicago and the other stores regularly, but the base of operations would stay here."

Olivia raised her eyebrows. It could work. On one condition. "Maybe. But I don't want any part of buying buildings out from under business owners. From now on, if we expand, we do it with new or vacant buildings. No one will be forced out. And we are equal partners with equal say. My business does not have the capitalization of yours, but I have my nationally syndicated show, the web presence, and the book."

Alex didn't hesitate. "Agreed."

They stared at each other. Olivia's face was flushed and Alex's grey eyes sparkled. "Do we have a deal?" he asked.

Olivia felt something shift inside. "Deal," she said softly, wondering what Harry and Gilberta would say. And Dan…

Alex put his cup down and reached for Olivia' hand. "This is the beginning of wonderful."

What have I just done, wondered Olivia, staring at the hand holding hers.

Olivia said very little as they cleaned up breakfast. Alex came over and lifted her chin up with one finger. She looked into the slate eyes that were full of love and promise. "It's a lot to think about," he whispered kissing her gently. "Can we talk more tonight? I could take you out to an early dinner, since we both have to work tomorrow."

Olivia put her arms around his waist, stood on her toes, and kissed him hard. "I would like that. What if you pick me up at six?"

"Six it is. Right now I have to get home and take care of Buster, whose legs are probably crossed."

With a final kiss, Alex left to make phone calls to set the plan in motion. They had agreed that Olivia would call Dan to set up a meeting to work out the partnership agreement. She glanced at the clock and realized it was already one in the afternoon. Taking a deep breath, she called Dan. He picked up on the second ring.

"Hey! How did the wedding go? I was thinking about you all day yesterday, but didn't want to disturb you by calling."

"It went very well, with only one problem that we were able to fix," she said, glossing over the cake drama. "At times, it was magical. I haven't debriefed with Claire yet, but last night she seemed very happy."

"We'll need to get together so you can tell me all the nitty-gritty details. Hopefully you can take today off to rest."

"I can." She hesitated. "Dan, I have something to tell you and a question to ask."

He heard something in the tone of her voice. "What's up?"

Olivia didn't know how to start. She knew it was going to sound crazy, saying it out loud.

"Are you still there?" asked Dan, wondering what was going on.

"I'm here. You probably won't believe what I'm about to say, but here goes. Alex and I have decided to form a partnership and we were wondering if you could draw up the papers."

Dan was stunned into silence.

"Dan?"

"Wow. I didn't see that coming! When did you decide this?"

"This morning."

"This morning? When did you have time to see him...," his voice trailed off as he began to realize what must have happened.

"He came over after the wedding...and stayed until just a little while ago."

Dan tried to gather his thoughts. "Again, wow!" He had always trusted Olivia's judgement, but he wondered if the emotional toll of the wedding and exhaustion had clouded it this time. "Can I ask how this came about?"

Olivia blushed. "We've been attracted to each other for some time, but our businesses kept us apart. Last night that didn't matter. This morning we decided to work it out, and we think we've come up with a solution."

"Do you love him?"

Olivia didn't know how to answer that. She loved being with him last night. She loved his scent and the feel of him. She loved cooking breakfast with him. She feared what this meant for her business; for herself as an independent woman. "I might. It's been so fast and the businesses complicate things."

"I need some time to absorb this. What if we meet Tuesday morning to talk over what this partnership would mean? Should I call Alex to ask him to join us at the office, or would you like to call him? We could meet around ten."

"I'll call him. Thanks, Dan.

"Olivia, I know I have no right to ask, but are you sure about this?"

"Honestly, I'm scared, but I think it's what I want to do. Let's see where we are on Tuesday."

"See you Tuesday. Let me know if anything changes."

"I will. See you then." She ended the call and sat on the window bench looking out into the calm, sunny afternoon. With Alex there the plan seemed right. In his absence, all her worries returned. Maybe Dan was right to question her; maybe she should slow things down. How would Harry and Gilberta take the news? Would she have the same level of creative independence working with such a big company? Looking out into the sunshine, she decided her usual tromp through the woods would help clear her mind.

Her walk and a nap calmed her down a bit, though she still felt unsettled. There remained many unanswered questions. Would she be able to work with Alex? It was one thing to have a relationship, it was another entirely to work all day with someone, then see them at night. Would their staff members work well together? Though, it could turn out to be a good thing for Harry and Gilberta. And what about Kaiya? She had just hired her as her business manager and she was fabulous. Where did she fit in?

By the time Olivia opened the door to Alex's knock, her mind was spinning again.

Alex looked at Olivia in her trim pants and lacy tunic, her hair tucked up in a chignon. She looked even more beautiful than before, if that were possible, but it was the stress in her eyes that concerned him. "Is everything okay?" he asked, caressing her cheek.

"Nothing's wrong, but I have lots of questions whirling in my brain. I'm scared, Alex. Scared of what I'm doing to myself; scared of what I'm doing to my friends."

Alex looked at her seriously. "I think I've dreamed of this so long that it seems right to me, but I can understand how you might not see it the same way. Let's talk about it when we get to the restaurant. Okay?"

Olivia smiled faintly. "Okay."

A bark came from the open window of Alex's car. "Oh, by the way," Alex started, looking a little sheepish. "Buster was not very happy with me when I came home today. Is there any way he can stay here while we're at dinner?"

Olivia looked at the chiseled face and the eyes that, rather than glinting steel, were filled with warmth. Her body tingled as she remembered last night. She wanted Alex with her tonight. She nodded her head and laughed. "Yes, he can stay. You have an interesting way of inviting yourself over for the night."

Alex grinned, then lowered his head for a quick kiss. "We better get going before I decide to skip dinner."

Alex settled Buster in the house before driving them over to the Italian restaurant where he had made reservations.

They sipped chianti companionably as they waited for their plates of wild mushroom risotto to arrive. Soft music played in the background. Luckily, Olivia did not see any of her customers in the dining room. She did not feel like being overheard or having to make small talk tonight. She looked at Alex, who had not taken his eyes off her all evening.

"Alex, what happens if something goes wrong with our relationship? What happens to the businesses?"

"Nothing will go wrong with our relationship; I'll make sure of that."

"Alex…you know there never is a guarantee when it comes to relationships."

"True, but I know my heart and I've lived enough to know what I want, and I want you. The question is…what do you want?"

Olivia caught her breath. Slowly, the words came out. "I want you right now, too, but what's really important is that I want to know that you will be there in thirty years to dance with me at a wedding."

Alex put his glass down and took Olivia's hand in his. "I promise you, if I'm still alive and kicking, that I will gladly dance with you in thirty years. I love you."

Olivia's eyes glistened with unshed tears. "I love you, too."

They couldn't tell how much time had gone by when the waiter arrived with their plates. Startled, they laughed shakily as the waiter put their plates down. Olivia was the first to speak. Once she started, she couldn't stop. All her worries came tumbling out.

"Let's make sure the contract has something in there anyway about how to deal with the business if something does happen. Another thing I was worrying about this afternoon is what will happen to my staff? Will Kaiya, my new business manager, have a position in the business? I do not want to lay anyone off and I don't want anyone demoted. If anything, I want my crew to have more opportunities and better pay. Will I have the same control over menus and pricing as I do now? What happens to your corporate chef? Who has responsibility for what? How do we…"

"Whoa!" Alex laughed. "Let's take this one at a time. I'm thinking that at the beginning, not a lot has to change, except that the European Gourmet name would disappear from the store and Sweet Sage would go back up."

"If the store has my business name on it, I'm going to feel responsible for the quality of the food in the cases. How would your corporate chef feel about working with me?"

"I haven't spoken to him about any of this, but you may be surprised at how good he is. As the co-owner of the business, you'll have the control, but you may find that you enjoy working with him. I see you as being a creative director of sorts. You need time to work on the show, recipes, books, and anything else you want to work on. I don't think you should be locked into the everyday production."

Olivia felt a glimmer of the familiar excitement of a new venture. "And where does Harry fit in? You already have a catering director."

"True, though honestly, I think Harry is far superior in terms of staff, training, and ambience. My catering director could be the sales manager, while Harry remains the director."

"Won't that cause hurt feelings?"

"It may, but I think when you are in business, you can't avoid all hurt feelings."

Olivia looked at Alex. She knew he was right. "Okay, I'll give you that one. What about Kaiya? I just hired her as my business manager and in less than two weeks she has whipped things into shape and jumped right in. Where does she belong?"

"Well, I let the original manager of this store go when things started out too slowly, so I'm doing the managing, which is not really where I should be focusing my energies. I'm not sure Kaiya would want to take on the store as well as what she is doing for you, but it would be great if she could. If things go well, we could always move her into a broader position for the company. It would be great if she could take a look at the managerial structure of the company and come up with some ideas on how to revamp it for efficiency. The company has grown and with our merger, it's going to look completely different. Her fresh eyes might be just the thing we need."

Olivia nodded as she sat over her plate of cold risotto. "Wow...so this is really happening..." she whispered.

"Only if you want it to happen. I know I'm excited, but I've been dreaming about this a lot longer than you have even given it a thought. I've had a chance to think about how we could begin the merger, but that doesn't mean that's the way it's going to happen. This is your company, too,...if we go through and do it. By the way, one of the phone calls I had to make today was to my parents. They are shareholders in the company, so I felt they needed to know what might be happening. I have complete control of the company and have the right to conduct business as I see fit, but felt it was only right to let them know."

Olivia's eyes widened. Of course! It was a private company started by his family! How would they accept her share in the ownership?

"And...?"

"I explained everything about you, how I felt about you, and what I intended to do with the business. They were happy for me and approved of the merger. They've seen your show, so knew who I was talking about. They said it would be a perfect marriage."

Olivia ignored that last word. She ate a couple of bites of her dinner, but her stomach was not interested in food. Alex managed to eat half of his before setting his fork down.

"How would you feel about going home? We both have to work tomorrow, and honestly I'm not hungry," suggested Olivia.

"That sounds like a fantastic idea," said Alex.

Alex took care of Buster before coming up to Olivia's bedroom to find her already tucked under the blankets. Sitting down on the side of the bed, he asked "How would you like a one-armed back rub?"

Olivia smiled and pulled him tenderly down to her for a long kiss. "A quick one," she replied smiling.

Chapter 39

The next day proved to be busy. Harry met the rental company at the Austin estate early in the morning to make sure everything was picked up and accounted for before he came by Sweet Sage for the debrief with the rest of the team. Olivia had decided to tell the team that day of the decisions she had made with Alex, but waited for Harry to get back before dropping the bombshell. Her stomach twisted with nervousness as she listened to Kaiya and Gilberta discuss what had been used for the wedding and whether the staff had been adequate.

Gilberta looked at Olivia. "Are you still worried about what happened with the cake Saturday? You seem distracted."

Olivia looked at her. It was incredible to believe, but that story seemed like a minor blip in the weekend. "I'm sorry Gilberta, I just have other things on my mind. When Harry comes back we'll talk about it."

Gilberta and Kaiya looked at her quizzically. "Anything we should worry about?" asked Kaiya.

"No, I don't think so," she replied. "By the way, does Harry know the cake story? I haven't told him, yet."

"I haven't talked to him since the wedding," Gilberta said turning to Kaiya. "Did you say anything to him after we left?"

"No. We were busy and I didn't think it was my place to say anything."

Olivia nodded. "We'll tell him when he comes in. Hopefully he won't be too upset. He did such a great job with the service. Even Edward was impressed!"

"Edward!" exclaimed Gilberta. "What a pain he was to work with. Will he be there this afternoon at the meeting with Claire?"

"Yes, but I think he has a different attitude now. You know, he might be important to us. He could bring business our way. I know he was a pill, but I think half of it was his own insecurity. I really think he liked working with us."

"Hmph!" grunted Gilberta with disgust. "You're definitely more charitable than I am."

Olivia laughed as Harry walked in the door. "What's so funny?" he asked.

"Olivia thinks Edward is the way he is because he's insecure and that he could bring us more business because he liked working with us," explained Gilberta.

"I hate to admit it, but after all his nagging and griping, he did do a good job and was very pleasant with the staff as we were cleaning up. You might be right," he nodded to Olivia as he took a seat around the table. He grabbed a slice of warm blueberry coffeecake that Olivia set in the center of the table while Kaiya poured coffee for everyone. "So how is everyone this morning? Rentals are all picked up with nothing missing and the tent people are breaking down the tents as we speak, so I feel great. That was a hell of a wedding, if I do say so myself."

Everyone nodded in agreement. Kaiya took out her phone to show some of the photos she had taken. "I've never seen anything like it. It was like a magical fairytale; it was so beautiful. Look how beautiful it looked in the sunset." Everyone gathered around the phone as she swept through the pictures. A picture of the cake flew by, and she quickly moved on to the next.

"Hey, wait a minute," Harry exclaimed. "I knew there was something I wanted to ask. What happened to the cake? I thought it was supposed to have five tiers, and I don't remember setting the cake table up with a riser."

The three women looked at each other. "What?" asked Harry, looking at them in bewilderment.

"Are you ready for a crazy story?" asked Kaiya.

"Yes…" replied Harry slowly.

Olivia recounted the events ending with what Alex had told her later that night. Harry turned pale and silently listened.

"Holy cow, Olivia! I knew Alex came back with the cake, but I never imagined that that's what happened to him!" exclaimed Gilberta.

"Harry, are you okay?" Olivia asked taking his hand.

"I'm so sorry…" he began.

"No! This had nothing to do with you and everything ended up beautifully. I'm not even sure Claire or Ella noticed the difference. So, I don't want to hear anymore 'I'm sorrys' from you. As a matter of fact, something very good came of it,"

Harry looked at her. "Is this 'something very good' that Tommy is now in jail?"

All three looked at Olivia as she blushed.

"Olivia? Did something happen between you and our hero, Alex?" Harry guessed.

Olivia nodded and took a deep breath. "I have a lot to tell you guys this morning. Alex came over to my place after the wedding."

Harry's eyebrows rose.

"We ended up talking about everything," she went on ignoring the looks from her three friends, "and came to an understanding."

"Is this a good understanding?" Gilberta asked.

"I think so, and I hope you will, too"

"Okay, you're being way too mysterious. Are you talking about dating Alex here, or something else?" Harry asked.

"Both." Olivia took a deep breath, then continued. "Yes, I'm seeing Alex and…we've decided to join our businesses, with Sweet Sage taking over the store."

Harry's jaw dropped and Gilberta and Kaiya looked stunned. Olivia looked at them with concern. "This will be good for all of us," she tried to assure them. "You'll all keep your positions and more, if you want it. Nothing changes in terms of the show, our books, the web, or how we do things. The only thing that changes, is that we will be part of something much bigger."

Harry was the first to speak. "How can you be so sure of that?"

"Because those were my first concerns, too. The contract will stipulate these conditions. This business would not exist without you, Harry and Gilberta. We've come too far together. I wouldn't give that up for the world." Turning to Kaiya, she added, "I know you came on board recently, but you are now part of the family and your position is also secure. As a matter of fact, it could grow, if you were interested." Turning back to the others, she said, "Both of you will have more opportunities to go in the directions you want to go in."

There was silence for a moment, then Olivia spoke. "You guys have taken so many risks this past year by hanging in there with me. Can you see your way to taking one more risk?"

Gilberta looked directly at Olivia. "Olivia, I'm willing to take the leap, but I do have one question for you. What happens if you and Alex don't see eye to eye and break off your relationship? Have you thought of that? What happens to the business then?"

"Fair question and yes, we've thought of that. Our share of the business will be exactly half of the entire company. The contract will stipulate an equitable split under those circumstances…but I don't think it will happen. I know this seems sudden to you, but it's been a while coming."

"Holy cannoli!" Harry exclaimed. "And I thought life was plenty exciting already!"

"We have a meeting with Claire and Edward at one. Why don't you three take a break and meet me back here a little before then and we'll drive over together. That way, you can process all of this and we can talk again later."

Kaiya looked at the other two. "I'm pretty clear on where I stand. I'm good for it. Right now I'd like to go sort out the wedding accounting."

Harry and Gilberta looked at each other. "I have to look at what's left in the walk-ins and you need to get ready for your show this week," Gilberta said looking at Olivia.

"And I need to figure out staff hours and go back to check on the tent breakdown," added Harry.

Olivia's eyes glistened with tears. She was the luckiest woman alive.

Before splitting off to their various projects, the four reviewed the wedding and made notes for further improvements. The chatter was music to Olivia's ears.

The meeting with Claire went easily. She had not noticed the difference in the cake. The evening had been such a success and her daughter had been so happy, that details escaped her notice. Edward, on the other hand, had notice…but decided to keep quiet. After the meeting, he approached Olivia and her friends as they were getting into the Sweet Sage truck. "I don't care what happened to the cake, and I don't want to know. I just want to let you know Sweet Sage will be one of my top recommendations in the future. It's been a pleasure working with you and your team," he said nodding to Harry and Gilberta.

Harry's eyebrows went up, then he reached over Olivia to shake Edward's hand. "You know, we started out with a bump, but I've got to say you've got style."

Edward smiled at the three. "Till we meet again."

When Olivia arrived home that evening, Buster greeted her at the door with his usual goofy smile. Olivia's heart filled nearly to bursting with a joy she had forgotten existed as she knelt and scratched behind his ears. Her golden kitchen was filled with life and soon she would have Alex home to talk to about everything that had happened to her that day.

Epilogue

Olivia glanced up at the chubby baker boy clock hanging on the brick wall. Six thirty. Her eyes swept the store that still buzzed with customers. It officially was closing time, but there were too many customers to close the door. She walked over to the bakery case and watched as a young man cleaned out the bottom of the empty case. It had been a very good Christmas Eve. Sales had far surpassed those from last year. She felt an arm encircle her waist, as she stood contemplating all that had happened in the last year.

Looking up, she met Alex's wide grin with a smile of her own.

"I knew we could conquer the world working together," he teased.

"Sure. I just had to tame you a little, that's all," retorted Olivia.

"Hey. All's fair in love and business."

She rolled her eyes and shook her head. "Not so much, kiddo"

Alex laughed.

Just then, Harry, looking poised and dapper in an Italian suit, came up to them with Edward in tow. "What do you say? Should we start locking some of the doors and hinting that we are closing?"

"Sounds like a good idea," Alex responded.

Olivia looked over to Edward. "Did you find what you wanted to get?" she asked.

"Yes," he answered with a meaningful look at Harry.

Harry blushed, then looked at his best friend. "I was going to wait to tell you, but I can't wait. We've decided to get married."

"Oh, Harry! Congratulations! Edward, I'm so happy for you!" Olivia exclaimed.

Harry looked at her hard. "You mean you approve?"

"Of course, but you don't need my approval! You couldn't have chosen a nicer person," she said giving each a hug.

"Congratulations," echoed Alex shaking hands with them.

Harry looked at Edward. "Let's go tell Gilberta and Kaiya. I'm just too happy to keep it inside!"

Edward smiled and allowed Harry to lead him off to the upstairs office to find his friends.

The store was quiet now. Customers and staff had all gone home to their friends and families. Alex and Olivia stood silently together for a few minutes before leaving, surveying the long golden expanse of their business. Alex turned and put his hand on the growing bump on Olivia's stomach. "You must be tired. One baby has been put to bed, now it's time for the other to take a rest."

Olivia covered his hand with hers and gazed into the eyes she had come to trust above all.

"Alex, will you marry me?"

Alex stood stunned for a second, then grabbed her in his arms and kissed her hard. "I thought you'd never ask."

Olivia laughed and went back to the business of kissing.

Made in the USA
Charleston, SC
17 November 2016